"Go away, Jake. This has nothing to do with you," Amy said.

"Are you saying this is *not* my baby?"

"No, she *is* your baby. But if it bothers you, go away. Forget you ever met me."

He stared at her. Was she serious?

"You said you don't do commitment, Jake. I promise that you're not committed to me or my baby. Financially or emotionally."

She crossed to the door and opened it.

Standing on the threshold, his thoughts in turmoil, Jake realized that he didn't want to go. He just didn't know how to stay. He headed for the gate. If she was bluffing, well, he was calling her.

The door clicked shut and he swung round, taken by surprise.

She really meant it!

Well, that was just fine. So did he. Now they both knew where they stood.

What happens when you suddenly discover your happy twosome is about to be turned into a...*family?*

Do you panic?
Do you laugh?
Do you cry?
Or...do you get married?

The answer is all of the above—and plenty more!

Share the laughter and the tears as these unsuspecting couples are plunged into parenthood! Whether it's a baby on the way, or the creation of a brand-new instant family, these men and women have no choice but to be

When parenthood takes you by surprise!

Look out in October for
Claiming His Baby #3673
by Rebecca Winters

THE BACHELOR'S BABY
Liz Fielding

HARLEQUIN®

TORONTO • NEW YORK • LONDON
AMSTERDAM • PARIS • SYDNEY • HAMBURG
STOCKHOLM • ATHENS • TOKYO • MILAN • MADRID
PRAGUE • WARSAW • BUDAPEST • AUCKLAND

ISBN 0-373-03666-3

THE BACHELOR'S BABY

First North American Publication 2001.

Copyright © 2001 by Liz Fielding.

This edition published by arrangement with Harlequin Books S.A.

® and TM are trademarks of the publisher. Trademarks indicated with
® are registered in the United States Patent and Trademark Office, the
Canadian Trade Marks Office and in other countries.

Visit us at www.eHarlequin.com

Printed in U.S.A.

PROLOGUE

JAKE HALLAM couldn't take his eyes off her. She arrived late for the christening, caught in one of the showers that had been chasing across the valley all day, and as she walked towards him a sudden shaft of sunlight lit up in the raindrops that clung to her.

They sparkled against the silver-grey velvet cloak that swirled around her ankles. Sparkled on the spray of flowers she was carrying. Sparkled on long dark lashes that curtained her eyes.

Then she pushed back the wide hood of her cloak and the sun, slanting through the stained glass of the old church, lit up the short, elfin cut of her pale blonde hair.

The baby, nestling in his mother's arms, whimpered restlessly and the newcomer leaned over, touched his cheek. 'Hello, gorgeous,' she cooed softly, in a voice like melted chocolate. The infant's complaint was immediately transformed into a smile.

And then she looked up, straight into his eyes, and repeated the soft, 'Hello'. Even without the 'gorgeous' tag, he felt the same instant desire to grin as she offered him a slender hand. 'I'm Amaryllis Jones.'

'Amaryllis?'

'That's just for formalities,' she said gravely. 'Now we've been introduced you may call me Amy.' He would have done, if he could have caught his breath. 'And you're Jacob Hallam. Willow and Mike have told me all about you.'

'It's Jake,' he said quickly. 'And whatever Willow

and Mike have told you—' he bit back the denial as he remembered where he was '—is probably true.'

'Really?' The corners of her mouth tucked into a small, teasing smile as she tilted her head thoughtfully to one side. 'I wonder. So few people live up—or down—to their reputations.'

Even as he struggled to remind himself that he was in church, godfather to the infant about to be baptised and with no business to be thinking the kind of thoughts that were racing through his head, she turned away to kiss Willow, the baby's mother, and apologise for her lateness.

'I noticed the bluebells in the orchard as I was leaving. They're just the colour of Ben's eyes so I stopped to pick some.'

That was all. Normality returned. Amy took baby Ben from his mother. The vicar ushered them towards the font and Jake thought he must have imagined the spark of something hot and sweet that had crossed the space between himself and Amy. An unspoken promise that said... Not now. Later.

As if she'd read his mind Amaryllis Jones lifted her lashes, flickered a sideways glance at him.

Her eyes weren't blue. They were green and ocean-deep and he was suddenly out of his depth and floundering. It was an unfamiliar sensation and every instinct warned him that he should head for the door while he still could. But he was keeping a promise he'd made to stand as godfather to Mike and Willow's first child and escape wasn't an option.

Yet all through the service Jake was distracted by the scent of the flowers she carried. It wove a spell through his mind so that all through the tea that followed, and the champagne and the toasts to baby Ben's health and

LIZ FIELDING 7

happiness, he was intensely aware of her presence shimmering on the edge of his consciousness. Once the photographs had been taken, and escape was possible, they had circled the company, keeping the maximum distance between them as if by unspoken agreement, understanding that to be close was to risk instant conflagration.

But when he'd glanced in her direction he'd had the feeling that he'd just missed meeting her gaze. Maybe it was simply his imagination working overtime. Maybe. Yet without a word spoken, without a gesture or so much as a lift of a brow, they arrived at the door at the same time, ready to leave.

'Hold on, Amy, it's raining again,' Mike said, as he walked them to the door. 'You'll get wet on your broomstick. I'll run you home.'

'Broomstick?' Jake repeated, turning to risk the heat of those dangerous eyes.

And for the first time since she'd arrived in church Amy met his gaze head-on. 'Mike thinks I'm a witch.' She should have been smiling. She wasn't. 'Don't you, Mike?' she asked, but her eyes continued to hold Jake prisoner.

Mike hesitated, and she tilted her head back and laughed, her throat a perfect white curve that Jake's hand ached to cradle. Then Willow called from the nursery and Amy said, 'You're needed, Mike.'

'Yes, but...'

'I'll take Amy home,' Jake said.

'You're quite sure? It's out of your way...'

'Quite sure.' He'd been going that way ever since Amy had looked at him. Maybe Mike was right. Maybe she was a witch.

'Oh. Right. Well, thanks... And thank you for today. Both of you. Give us a call when you get back from the

States, Jake. Come and stay.' Then, almost as an after-thought, Mike added, 'And take care.'

They paused on the doorstep and there was a moment of silence while Amy, her eyes level with his, regarded him thoughtfully. 'You're quite sure?' she asked after a moment, echoing Mike's words.

She wasn't talking about the lift.

Neither was he when he replied, 'Quite sure.' Jake led the way to his car, opened the door. Her cloak trailed over the edge and he bent to lift it, tuck it inside. The material was soft, sensual beneath his fingers. Silk velvet. Like a woman's skin. Maybe that was why his hands were shaking as he slid the key into the ignition. 'Which way?' he asked abruptly.

'Left.' He glanced at her. 'I live on the other side of the village. It's not far.'

Not far, but it was a different world. Mike and Willow's home was minimalist modern, a labour-saving miracle of architecture designed for busy people and set in a low maintenance courtyard garden with a small paddock beyond that was grazed by a neighbour's elderly pony.

Amy, in total contrast, lived in a piecrust cottage surrounded by an old-fashioned garden filled with spring flowers that bloomed with wild abandon. They spilled over onto the brick paths, splattering their legs with raindrops as they ran for the door.

Once they'd reached the shelter of the pitch-roofed porch they paused for breath. And to look at one another. Take a moment to consider. Nothing had been said, but they both knew that once he was beyond the front door all the thoughts that were now safely in their heads would spill over into unstoppable action; there would be no stepping back.

It was as if she was saying, You're quite sure? again.
But this time silently. His own silence was all the answer
she needed, and she held out her key to him. It hung
there between them, shimmering dull silver in the stormy
light, and at the back of Jake's mind warning bells began
to ring.

'I don't do commitment,' he said roughly. Almost
hoping that she would tell him to go. Leave. Get out.

She didn't say any of those things. She said nothing,
her green eyes holding his, demanding that he make his
own decision about whether to go or stay. The warning
bells clanged with a desperate urgency but all afternoon
her eyes had silently promised him everything he had
ever wanted from a woman. Promised that she would
fulfil his every dream.

She was wasting her time. He had no dreams. He was
a hollow man, rich in the stuff that money could buy,
but without a heart, incapable of love.

Most of the time he lived with it, scarcely noticing
the emptiness. Today, wrapped in the warmth of friends
whose love for each other, whose happiness had reached
new heights with the birth of their baby son, he had been
painfully aware of his own shortcomings.

Amy Jones was offering him a chance to forget, lose
himself for a few hours, and without a word he gathered
in key and woman in one movement. For a moment he
simply held her, breathed in the scent of rain-washed
earth and wallflowers and bluebells. For a moment anything seemed possible.

Fantasy, he knew, but his mouth came down on hers
with a deep hunger, a longing to be proved wrong.

CHAPTER ONE

FIRST MONTH. Your pregnancy will not have been confirmed yet. Many women, however, feel pregnant without knowing quite why.

AMY didn't need the test to confirm what her body was already telling her. What, in her mind, she already knew, had known from the moment when the early-morning sun had turned the world gold in a moment of pure magic.

Even before that.

She'd known how it would be in that first second when Jake had turned and watched her walk towards him. Known that this was the man she'd been waiting for. That this was the moment.

Afterwards Jake had held her, and although he'd said nothing she'd known that he, too, had felt something way beyond his expectations of a casual encounter with a woman he'd made it clear he was making no promises to see again. But she'd looked into his velvet-brown eyes and seen something beyond the moment. She'd seen fear, too.

He was afraid of this. Not just of giving, but of receiving love.

She smiled as she waited, remembering. He'd given generously. Far more than he'd intended. Now, maybe, she'd have to convince him that it was enough. Which might be more difficult. For both of them.

She glanced impatiently at her watch. Despite her certainty, she'd left her assistant to close up the shop and rushed home, impatient for chemical proof, to be reassured that hope and imagination weren't simply working overtime.

And now it was taking all her will-power not to stare at the little plastic wand, willing the blue line to appear and make it official.

The time waiting for the result of the test seemed far longer than the two weeks since Jake had left her bed. Said goodbye with a kiss that had somehow lingered and, in that golden dawn, had deepened and erupted into something else entirely before he'd dragged himself back to reality and raced away to catch a plane without so much as an 'I'll call you' or 'I'll see you' to suggest he'd be back. She'd expected nothing else. Not from Jake.

He'd warned her. He didn't pretend.

Lying alone in the warm nest of her bed, listening as he'd moved swiftly through the cottage, snapped the door shut behind him as if to convince himself of the finality of his departure, heard his wheels spin against the gravel of the lane as he'd sped away from her, she had wondered what made him so afraid.

Wondered what had happened in the past to send him racing away from the warmth of a woman's arms, even when he'd plainly longed to stay.

Cross with herself for standing there, waiting for the test to develop, she put the wand down on the edge of the bath. She didn't need it. She had better things to do.

She opened the door to the small front bedroom she'd been using as an office. Her hand briefly touched her waist. She'd be working from home more in the future; she'd need her little office.

The other spare room was stacked with stock from her

shop. Boxes of handmade soaps, scented candles, essential oils. She'd have to rent more space from Mike, she decided as she looked about her, run her mail-order business from the craft centre.

She'd have to totally reorganise the shop, too. It was time to promote Vicki, give her more responsibility, take on someone else part-time. She was going to need help. A lot more help. A sudden tremor of doubt shivered through her. Suppose she couldn't cope on her own?

For a moment her hand touched her waist. No, not on her own. Never again. Her baby might be no bigger than a match-head, there might be nothing yet for the world to see, but inside her something amazing was happening. Already her baby had a backbone, a primitive heart...

The low afternoon sun was shining in through a window that overlooked the rear garden. Yes, this would make a perfect nursery. She could see it already...had the colours picked out in her mind...

And she stopped being cool and serious and totally in control and rushed back to the bathroom.

Yes!

Her hand was shaking as she snatched up the tester. A blue line. Did that mean it was a boy? No, no. Stupid. Of course it wasn't a boy. She was going to have a girl. She and Jake were going to have a baby girl.

Her legs went suddenly wobbly and she clutched at the sink and lowered herself onto the edge of the bath.

She was pregnant.

It wasn't just a feeling any more; it wasn't just something she 'knew'. It was fact. Not just some airy notion that couldn't, shouldn't be true. Jake wasn't a man to take risks. But that last time something extraordinary had happened and neither of them had thought of anything but a deep and desperate need to be held, to be loved. Without limitation, reservation, conditions attached.

And now there was a baby, his baby, their baby, growing inside her. A life begun. It was totally, seriously true.

A smile forced its way across her face, erupting into a disbelieving laugh that faded as quickly as it came.

Falling in love with Jake Hallam had not been a good move. Head-over-heels-at-first-sight falling in love was never a good idea, especially not with a man who'd made a point of explaining his attitude to commitment before he'd stepped over her threshold.

But it had been too late then.

She'd tried. She'd known it was pointless, but she'd made an effort and really tried. After that first moment, when their hands had touched and their gazes had locked and all kinds of incredible sensations had made concentration on anything else very, very difficult, she'd kept her distance. Kept the length of the room between them. She'd sensed that he was doing the same thing, unnerved by the certainty that their fates were inextricably linked.

Yet they had both arrived at the door at the same time, ready to leave. If they'd planned it, it couldn't have been better timed.

The only comfort was that he didn't know she was in love with him. Men distrusted that kind of emotional stuff. Not that he'd have believed her anyway. If she'd used the 'L' word, Jake would have panicked, certain that she'd cling. If she wasn't very careful, he'd see the baby as an attempt to entrap him.

Amy laid the flat of her palm against her stomach. No. He must never feel that. If he came back it must be because he wanted to. Because nothing could stop him.

She knew he'd try to stay away.

He'd found it too difficult to leave her not to recognise

the danger. He'd driven away from her cottage as if the
hounds of hell were on his back. Which was, she decided,
promising. It suggested a certain unease, a fear that saying
he 'didn't do commitment' wouldn't be enough.

He was mistaken. It would be. If he wanted it that
way. His decision.

She'd have to tell him about the baby, though. Before
he heard it from someone else. She had three or maybe
four months' grace, but after that it would be difficult to
hide the fact that she was pregnant, and Mike had seen
them leave together, had been aware of the tension between them.

His parting 'Take care' had been loaded with appre-
hension…As if he would have protected each of them
from the other, but had sensed the attempt was futile.

But once Mike knew about the baby it wouldn't put
a strain on his powers of deduction to put two and two
together and come up with the date of Ben's christening.

The phone began to ring and she let the thought go.
She had plenty of time before she had to worry about
Jake's reaction to fatherhood. He was in America, would
be gone for weeks. He'd stressed that. As if he needed
to reinforce the message. So, she had ages to work out
the best way to break the news to him.

Just for the moment it was her secret, and she planned
to keep it that way.

Then, as she headed for the door, she realised she was
still holding the little plastic spill. Even as her hand
moved towards the wastebin she discovered she was totally incapable of throwing away the precious evidence
of her baby's existence. Instead she popped it into a little
glass jar standing on the bathroom windowsill and went
to deal with her call.

*　　*　　*

'Jake? Are you happy with that?'

Jake had been miles away. Thousands of miles away. His body might be sitting in a boardroom in downtown New York, but his mind was on the other side of the Atlantic. Suddenly, he couldn't get Amaryllis Jones out of his mind.

He'd done a pretty good job of it during the last month. He wasn't quite sure why, but he sensed it would be a wise move to forget all about her.

Okay, so he hadn't been able to totally eradicate the searing memory of the way they'd been together. But working hard on setting up a partnership with an American telecommunications company whose CEO had been determined to give him the VIP treatment had made it relatively easy—or, if not easy, at least possible—to push her right to the back of his mind.

But now, sitting with their massed lawyers hammering out the final details, nailing down any loose ends, all he could think of was the scent of bluebells and rain on warm English soil, a woman's touch that had seemed to reach down into his soul.

What on earth had possessed him? They'd been at a christening, for heaven's sake! He was the baby's god-father!

Was that it? An atavistic yearning for fatherhood sending him over the edge? No way! He enjoyed being godfather to Ben but that was as close to fatherhood as he ever intended to get.

It was why he was so careful to choose his partners with a detachment that bordered on coldness. He didn't walk, he ran from any possibility of emotional entanglements. He kept his relationships uncomplicated, the kind he could walk away from without a backward glance.

Love was too easy to say, too difficult to mean. He'd learned that the hard way.

The only person in the world who'd ever been there for him had been his foster mother. Aunt Lucy was a great lady and he owed her a lot, would be grateful to her until his dying day, but he still knew, deep down, that it wasn't him she cared for.

She opened her heart to any needy child, or puppy, or kitten who hadn't got anywhere else to go. He had been just one of dozens through the years. She was kind, warm-hearted, totally honest. It was in her nature to take in the heartsore strays, put them back on their feet, head them in the right direction and despatch them into the world. She'd done it for him, saved him from the kind of trouble a hurting youth could all too easily succumb to, but he wasn't fooling himself. It hadn't been personal.

And observing Aunt Lucy had taught him the wisdom of keeping a certain protective distance between himself and the risk of pain. Only someone you loved could hurt you.

With Amy Jones alarm bells had rung right on cue, every instinct warning him to stay away. And he had. Kept his distance. But they'd still arrived at the door together as if they'd planned it. Maybe she had. Maybe Mike was right. Maybe Amy had looked at him with those wide green eyes and bewitched him. Nothing else could account for the way he was feeling. Nothing else could account for the fact he couldn't get her out of his mind.

'Jake? Do we have a deal?'

He dragged himself back to the air-conditioned chill of the boardroom, looked around the table at the men waiting for his decision and realised that he hadn't heard a word anyone had said for the last ten minutes. Not a great way to do business. Not the way he did business.

Standing up, he closed the folder in front of him and said, 'Thanks for your time, gentlemen. I'll let you know.'

Before anyone had registered that the meeting was over, he was out of the room and using his cellphone to book himself on the next flight back to London.

Amy was working in the garden when she heard footsteps coming round the cottage. She looked up and smiled as she saw Willow Armstrong pushing Ben along the path in his new, all-terrain buggy.

'Wow! Fancy wheels, Ben!'

'A present from a doting grandpa,' Willow said, with a grin.

A grandpa. Her baby wouldn't have a grandpa. Or a grandma. Not even an aunt to call her own. 'Lucky Ben,' she said softly.

'Am I interrupting something vital?' Willow asked, looking at the half-dug trench. 'Only I haven't seen you since the christening.' She paused, as if waiting for Amy to offer some exciting reason for her lack of sociability.

'Is it that long?' she hedged. As if she hadn't counted every hour, every day of four long weeks, waiting for Jake to return—the last two searching for the perfect words to break the news of his impending fatherhood. 'The garden seems to take up every spare minute at this time of year.'

'Yes, well, I'm here to interrupt you. It's such a lovely evening I thought I'd give the buggy a test run on the common while Mike gets the dinner. Catch up with the gossip and with luck get a cup of tea into the bargain?'

Amy jabbed her spade into the soft earth and joined her visitors on the path. The baby was lying beneath the canopy shading him from the sun, a little tuft of fair hair sticking up on his forehead. He was gorgeous. Perfect. Without thinking her hand flew to her waist where her own baby was growing, unseen, unknown.

'It's lovely to see you,' she said, snatching off her gardening gloves before Willow had a chance to register the giveaway gesture, hoping that the flash of heat in her cheeks would be put down to nothing more than exertion. She wasn't ready to share her news yet. Not even with Willow. Not until she'd told Jake. 'I've been meaning to drop by,' she said quickly, 'but I've been reorganising the shop, and if I don't get my beans in now…' Leaving a summer bereft of the delights of home-grown runner beans to her friend's imagination, she took the handle of the buggy and began to push it towards the door. 'But I'm ready for a break. Come inside so I can wash my hands and give this little angel a cuddle.'

Ben began to fidget and his face crumpled as he began to grizzle. Willow bent over him and picked him up. 'Er, I think I'd better change him before you get too close, Amy.'

'Do you need a hand?' Had she sounded too eager? Too keen? 'Not that I know one end of a baby from the other,' she added quickly.

'It's a sharp learning curve, believe me,' Willow said, wrinkling her nose. 'Maybe you should start with something less demanding.'

'Maybe you're right. Maybe I should just go and put the kettle on. You know where the bathroom is. Help yourself.'

*   *   *

'Jake! What a surprise. Come on in.' Mike watched as Jake paid off the taxi and then said, 'I thought you were still in the US.'

'I was. Until last night.' His bag was at his feet and he was holding a small carrier. 'I bought this for Ben.'

'And you've come straight from the airport? It must be something pretty special.' Mike took the carrier, glanced at the contents and then looked up. 'A teddy?'

'It's an American teddy.' Jake realised that as a reason for his dash from the airport it was pretty feeble. He couldn't think what had possessed him to buy it. Except he'd seen it sitting there, in the airport shop, while he'd been waiting for his flight to be called and he'd thought… 'Press its paw and it plays Yankee Doodle.'

He couldn't remember why it had seemed like a good idea at the time. He didn't do fluffy toys. He didn't see the point in them. He was the down-to-earth, practical man who'd given his new godson blue chip stock for his christening present. After all, what use was a silver mug? It would just make work and collect dust.

Mike took out the bear, regarded the stars-and-stripes bow tie and waistcoat and grinned. 'It was a great idea if it brought you down to see us.' The welcome was warm, and if he wasn't totally convinced by the reason for the visit he kept his thoughts to himself. 'Willow will love him.'

'Great.' Jake practically cringed with embarrassment. What on earth was he doing?

'Well, don't stand on the doorstep, man. If you've just flown back from the States you must be fit to drop.'

'No, I'm intruding. I should have rung first…' Jake stopped, suddenly unsure of himself. He didn't do stuff like this, drop in unannounced, buy toys. Let his attention wander in meetings.

'Nonsense. Willow's taken Ben for a walk, but she won't be long and she'll be thrilled to bits to see you. And since she'll insist you stay, you might as well take your bag upstairs right now. You know the way.'

Jake dragged a hand over his face. 'You're quite sure?' He frowned as the words echoed in his head, as if someone had just said them a moment before. 'I don't know why I came. I should have gone straight home—'

Again Mike's look suggested he was fooling himself. Again he tactfully kept his thoughts to himself. 'Jake, you're a friend, you're welcome any time. Why don't you grab a shower while I put some coffee on? Are you hungry? Or can you wait for dinner?'

'A shower and coffee sound perfect.'

'Ten minutes?'

'Mike—' Mike, heading for the kitchen, paused and looked back. On the point of asking about Amy, asking how she was, Jake stopped himself. 'Nothing. Just thanks.'

'Sure. Take your time.'

He picked up his bag, carried it up to the guest room and wasted no time getting under the shower. He should be tired. Instead he felt fired up, excited, eager as a puppy fresh from a nap. He switched the shower to cold and stood there while he counted to a hundred. Slowly. It made no difference.

He wandered back into the bedroom, towelling his hair as he gazed out over the fields at the back of the house. From the window he could see Willow hurrying along the footpath, pushing Ben in his buggy, eager to be home.

Marriage, families. He was a puzzled spectator, unable to understand why it worked for some people. It was as if he had a vital piece missing. As if, somewhere inside him, a light hadn't been switched on.

Amy Jones had switched on something, though. This was new. This eagerness. And the warning bells clanged ever more loudly, warning him that he should have stayed on the other side of the Atlantic until the feeling had passed.

As he turned from the window, pulled on a shirt and a pair of chinos, he heard Willow come in through the back door.

'Mike! I'm home.' Home. The word sliced through him like a knife-blade. He had a penthouse apartment that had cost telephone numbers overlooking the Thames, furnished by someone whose job it was to save him the bother of having to think about it. It was a showpiece. It was a declaration of his status. It was hardly a home. 'Where are you? You won't believe what I've got to tell you.'

He heard her go into the kitchen, her voice dropping as she found Mike. He shouldn't have come. It had been a mistake, he thought, as he let himself out of the bedroom.

'I'm telling you it's true, Mike. There's no mistake.' He paused on the stairs as Willow's voice rose again. 'Amy's pregnant.'

It was like stepping off a cliff.

'Willow…' Mike's voice was a sharp warning, but she didn't appear to notice.

'Up you come, sweetheart,' she said, picking up Ben before rattling on. 'She had that little thing—you know, the little plastic thing from the pregnancy test. I went upstairs to change Ben and it was there…right there in a pot on the windowsill in her bathroom.' She laughed. 'I did that, too. You teased me about it but I couldn't bear to throw it away. I needed to see it every day just to remind myself it was true…' Jake wasn't sure how he descended the remainder of the stairs. 'The blue line was a bit fuzzy but there isn't any doubt about it.'

'Did you say anything to her?'

'No, of course not. She'll tell me when she's ready and I'll act as surprised as anything.' Jake stood in the kitchen doorway and watched Willow, pink-cheeked with excitement from hurrying home with her news, blow into Ben's neck, making him giggle. A charming scene of domesticity that he saw, but had no way of understanding. 'The thing I can't work out is who the father could be. She's not a woman to make a mistake, so it must have been planned, but I didn't know she'd been involved with anyone recently…' She looked up, as if sensing something. 'Mike?'

Mike was looking right at him. He didn't need to guess who the father of Amy's baby was. He knew.

Willow, suddenly realising they weren't alone, spun round. 'Jake! I didn't see your car. Darling, how lovely to see you. Are you staying?'

'I…um…' He couldn't speak. Couldn't find his voice to say the words. This couldn't be happening.

'Jake's staying,' Mike said, helping him out. 'But I think right now he has something he needs to do. Why don't we go and put Ben to bed, hmm?'

Her forehead creased as she latched on to the sudden inexplicable tension, her gaze switching between Mike and Jake and then it clicked. For a moment she had trouble keeping her lower lip from hitting the floor until, with a supreme effort at self-control, she said, 'Good plan.'

Jake pushed open the gate, paused. The garden had moved on while he'd been away. The bluebells had faded and now lilac, thick with blossom, scented the air and a blackbird was singing from a high perch in an apple tree.

A small black cat blinked sleepy yellow eyes at him from a patch of catnip. And from the rear of the cottage he could hear Amy's voice raised in a lilting song that might have been a lullaby.

He refused to succumb to such seductive enchantment. He wasn't enchanted. He was mad, mad as hell, and Amy was about to hear all about it. He found her wielding a spade with an easy competence that suggested long practice; her gardening skills were clearly not confined to picking flowers.

She was wearing thick cord trousers and heavy boots that contrasted with the femininity of a broad-brimmed straw hat that shaded her face. And a man's shirt. What man?

She stopped, rubbed her sleeve across her face, leaving her cheek streaked with dirt, and he forgot about the shirt as anxiety squeezed the breath from his lungs. Should she be working like this? Digging?

'Should you be doing that?' he demanded harshly.

'If I want homegrown beans on my table, then yes,' she replied easily, no trace of surprise in her voice. 'But if you're volunteering, be my guest.' She pushed the spade into the soil, stepped back and turned to look at him. He needed, wanted to see into her eyes; the hat threw shade across her face, keeping her thoughts hidden. But her voice caught at him, drawing him closer.

Jake's voice was hard, angry. Amy had heard him open the gate, walk around the cottage, and had recognised footsteps last heard racing away from her.

She'd forced herself to carry on working, leaving him to speak first, even though she longed to leap up, fling herself into his arms and pull him inside the house so

that she could show him just how pleased she was to
see him, hoping he was feeling the same hot surge of
excitement, desire. She felt raw, unbridled pleasure that
he'd returned.

For a moment he took a step closer, as if he felt it
too, but then he stopped. The sun was low at his back
and his face was shadowed so that she couldn't see his
expression. Which was perhaps a good thing, if it
matched his voice.

'I thought you were still in America,' she said, when
the silence grew too long.

'I was. Now I'm back. Should you be doing that?' he
repeated. 'In your condition.'

Her condition? She felt the heat rise to her cheeks. He
couldn't know. There was no way on earth he could
know. Yet his voice, his repeated question, suggested
that somehow he did, and when she didn't answer he
turned abruptly and walked towards the rear door of the
cottage, pushed it open, ducking under the low lintel as
he went inside. Amy abandoned the bean trench for the
second time that afternoon and, pulling off her gardening
gloves, followed him.

He wasn't in the mud room or the kitchen. 'Jake?
Where are you?' she called, dropping her gloves, kicking
off her earth-caked boots. A creak from the floor above
her betrayed his whereabouts. What on earth…? 'Jake,
what are doing? What do you want?'

Upstairs, in the bathroom, Jake gripped the basin. This
couldn't be happening to him. It couldn't be true.
Fatherhood had no part in his life plan. He didn't want
this. No way. Never.

Except that it was. The evidence was apparently there,
right there, before his eyes.

His hand was shaking as he reached for the piece of

plastic with its telltale line of blue. He gripped it hard, wrapping it in his fist, wanting to break it, smash it, make it go away. Such a small thing. So insignificant. So easy to overlook.

He wouldn't have known what it was but for Willow. If he'd called in to see Amy...

If!

Who did he think he was fooling? He hadn't been able to wait to see her! All the teddies in the world couldn't hide the truth of that. He'd have come here and made hot, sweet love with her, then they'd have shared a shower, and with the evidence right in front of him he still wouldn't have known.

How long would she have waited to tell him? Until it was too late to do anything about it. '...not a woman to make a mistake, so it must have been planned...' was what Willow had said to Mike.

His hands bunched into fists and he banged them down on the white porcelain sink. How much had she planned? All of it? Even that dramatic last-minute entry at the christening?

She'd known he would be there, singled him out, enchanting him with her green eyes and seductive voice. And he didn't doubt for a minute she knew, understood exactly what effect she would have on any susceptible man.

Oh, yes. It had been planned, and, libido rampant, he'd fallen for it. Right down to that last magical embrace when her kiss had trawled him in, tempting him beyond thought...

What a fool! What an idiot!

What on earth had possessed him? He was a man with 'precaution' stamped on his brain. Mike had as good as warned him. 'Take care,' he'd said. He hadn't added,

'She'll bewitch you.' Not that it would have made any difference.

Jake had thought himself invulnerable to even the most meticulously planned guerilla attack on his heart. It had been tried before and his heart was totally immune to sentiments beyond his experience, beyond his understanding. Which was why he'd so cavalierly ignored the danger signals, Mike's warning.

So now what?

Did she believe that he would marry her because she was carrying his child? Had she picked out a millionaire daddy for her baby? Well, she'd picked the wrong man for those games.

'Jake?'

He turned as softly, oh, so softly, her voice caressed him, teased him, stole into every corner of his mind.

Take care.

Mike was right. Even now it was taking every ounce of self-control to stop himself from reaching out for her, from taking her into his arms, telling her that it would be all right.

He knew better.

He wasn't like Mike, who'd grown up in a warm, caring family and had learned to play happy families at his mother's knee. He'd warned Amy, told her that he didn't do commitment, and the sooner she understood that it would take more than a blue line on a stick of plastic to suck him into her tender trap, the better.

'Jake?' she repeated, the soft inflection inviting an explanation.

'Amy?' he responded, his voice lifting in ironic mimicry. And opened his hand so that she would know exactly what he meant. 'Now, I'll ask you again. Should you be digging in your condition?'

'I'm pregnant, Jake,' she said quietly, refusing to respond to the aggression in his voice. 'Not an invalid.'

'And you intend going through with it?' he demanded.

She regarded him steadily, sorrowfully, her eyes all too visible now, all too easy to read, and he dearly wished the words unsaid. Unthought.

'This is my baby, Jake. She might only be this big—' and she held her finger and thumb with scarcely a space between them '—but she's my little girl.' Then she turned and walked out of the bathroom.

Jake frowned, followed her down the stairs. 'You can tell that it's a girl? Already?' he demanded.

She shook her head impatiently. 'Go away, Jake. This is nothing to do with you.'

'Nothing…' His breath caught in his throat. 'Are you saying this is *not* my baby?' he demanded. If she was, the sick feeling that had been sitting like a stone in his stomach since Willow erupted into the kitchen with her news should have evaporated. It hadn't. It had shifted, changed, deepened. 'Well? Are you?'

'No, Jake, I'm not saying that. She's your baby. Our baby. What I'm saying is that you needn't…'

'What? I needn't what?'

'Worry about us.' Her hand hovered briefly at her waist, so that he would know which 'us' she was referring to, before she let it drop to her side. 'I don't need you to hold my hand. *We* don't need you. If it bothers you, just go away, forget you ever came here. Forget you ever met me.'

He stared at her. Was she serious? 'That's what you want?' She didn't answer him and he suddenly realised what was going on. She wanted a baby with a daddy rich enough to ensure that it lacked for nothing. She didn't want the trouble of a man about the house. 'I'll be hearing from your lawyers, is that it?' he asked, keeping his own voice flat and expressionless.

'Lawyers?' She shook her head, as if he was slow-witted or something. 'I don't want your money, Jake. I have money. I run a successful business…'

Yeah, sure. He wasn't that slow. 'You can't run a business with a baby on your hip.'

'Watch me.' Then she made the slightest of gestures, apparently dismissing him and his concerns. 'Or not. As you please. You said you don't do commitment, Jake. I heard you, and you can believe me when I promise that you're not committed to me or my baby. Financially or emotionally.' There was a crispness in her voice that suggested she was losing patience. 'And you needn't worry about what Mike and Willow will think. I'll speak to them. They know me; they'll understand.'

'Will they? I'm damned if I do.'

'No? Well, I'm sorry, Jake, I'm afraid I can't put it any plainer.'

And she crossed to the door, opened it as if she was setting free some small frightened creature that she was pushing out into the world for its own good.

Standing on the threshold, his thoughts in a turmoil, he realised that he didn't want to go. He just didn't know how to stay. And if he did stay it would give Amaryllis Jones entirely the wrong idea about his determination not to get caught up in the emotional rollercoaster she had boarded.

Bad idea.

Instead he headed for the gate while he still remembered how, determined not to look back once he'd got there. If she was bluffing, well, he was calling her.

The door clicked shut before he'd gone half a dozen steps and he swung round, taken by surprise.

Dammit, she meant it! She really meant it!

Well, that was just fine. So did he. Now they both knew where they stood.

CHAPTER TWO

SECOND MONTH. The tendency to put on weight begins. Morning sickness may begin to bother you now, although it won't necessarily be in the mornings. It's time to visit your doctor and maybe get a scan.

'YOUR dates suggest you shouldn't plan anything strenuous for the second half of December.' The doctor crossed to the sink to wash her hands.

'You mean I'll have to put the two weeks' skiing in Klosters on hold?' Amy asked, grinning stupidly. First intuition, then chemistry, and now medical science had confirmed that she was pregnant and she was grinning for Britain. Until she realised how snug her waistband had become. 'Uh, should I be putting on weight already, Sally?'

'I'm afraid so. You've had the fun; it's downhill all the way from here.'

'Downhill? I thought I was supposed to glow.'

'You will, my dear. You will. It's nature's compensation for the morning sickness, the heartburn, the loss of visual contact with your feet—'

'Okay, okay,' Amy said quickly. 'That'll do. I get the picture.'

'Do you?' Dr Sally Maitland turned and looked at her thoughtfully. 'Pregnancy is the easy bit. I'd be happier if I thought this wasn't going to be parenthood for one,' she said. 'That your baby's father...' she paused momentarily, but when no name was forthcoming carried on '…is planning on sticking around to see through what he started.'

That was the trouble with having a doctor who'd known you since she'd put you in your mother's arms. She didn't feel the need to be in the least bit tactful. As for the question…

It was a week since Jake had walked out of her cottage, called a cab on his mobile as he'd walked back to Mike and Willow's place and high-tailed it back to London with a face like thunder. She'd had the details from Willow, who'd raced over, full of remorse at her unintentional blunder.

'He's had a bit of shock,' she'd said, in an attempt to excuse his reaction to the news. 'It's all my fault, blurting it out like that to Mike. I am *so* sorry.'

'Don't worry about it, Willow. He'd have had to know sooner or later.'

'Later might have been better. When you'd had a chance to get to really know Jake. Find out what makes him tick beyond an insatiable capacity for work and a gift for making money.' She shrugged. 'No one else has a clue. Just that this kind of stuff is difficult for him. I believe he had a rough childhood, although he never talks about it. I get the impression that his mother abandoned him and commitment—'

'It's all right, Willow. Really.'

'We're still friends?'

'The best. I would have told you about the baby, but I wanted to tell Jake first. You saved me an awkward moment.'

'I doubt that,' she said. Then, 'Give him time to get his head round it. He'll be back.'

'Maybe.' She wasn't counting on it. Willow hadn't

been there. Hadn't heard the way he'd asked if she was 'going through with it.'

'Deep down he's a really caring man, Amy. He still helps out the woman who fostered him with her shop. I mean really helps. He could pay someone to do it, but he goes down there, makes sure she's coping, does her accounts. I've even seen him stacking shelves. Okay, so he lives for his work,' Willow admitted. 'Seven days a week, fifty-two weeks a year, but he found time to give us a hand when Mike and I were working on a charity project for deprived kids. He's never slow to put his hand in his pocket—'

'I'm not a charity case.'

'No, of course not. Well, give him time.'

But how much time? Amy wondered. He had something less than eight months, which seemed for ever right now, but the clock was running.

'Amy?' She snapped back to the present. To the doctor, who was waiting for some response from her. '*Is* the father going to be sticking around?'

'What? Oh. I don't know.' Which was something of a first for her. It was her ability to read people, feel their moods, understand their uncertainties that had made Mike look at her sideways more than once. This time she seemed to have got it all wrong. 'I just don't know.'

'Right. Well, in that case we'd better get down to practicalities.' Sally picked up the phone. 'Let's see how soon we can get a scan...'

Forget you ever met me.

He'd tried. For three weeks he'd been trying. Absolutely determined to wipe Amy Jones from his memory, he'd thrown himself into work. Work had always been the answer to the emptiness, and there was plenty of that to distract him now that the American deal had finally gone through.

Unfortunately, this time it wasn't working.

Amy might have told him to go away, forget about her and her baby, and she'd certainly sounded as if she'd meant it.

But it wasn't that easy. This was his worst nightmare, the kind that brought him awake sweating and shivering in the middle of the night. Forgetting was going to take a lot of effort. Absolute concentration.

For that he needed to wipe away all sense of unfinished business. Of concern. At least the rewards of hard work provided the means to assuage the guilt that was gnawing at him, that would continue to gnaw at him while he worried about how she would cope. Well, he could deal with that.

He regarded the cheque he had written with a certain amount of satisfaction. He might suffer from emotional attachment deficit but he had no doubt that Amy could provide enough emotion for two; he'd had the most vivid experience of her ability to connect, to enfold, to touch. Just the touch of her fingertips on his face had been…

'They're waiting for you in the boardroom, Jake.' His secretary's disembodied voice on the intercom dragged him back from the heat of his memories. He should have known. Anyone who could give that much would always be a threat to his detachment. His peace of mind. And she would expect something in return. All he had was money.

'I'll be right there, Maggie,' he said. And he signed the cheque. Amy could do the warm, emotional stuff and he would pay the bills. Between them, the baby wouldn't lack for anything.

He stuffed the cheque in an envelope, addressed it and

tossed it into his out tray. Now he could get on with the one thing he understood—making money—and forget all about Amy Jones.

He'd been in the meeting for less than ten minutes when the envelope lying in his out tray began to niggle at him, distracting him. He should have enclosed a note…he should have said something. That he was sorry. That he—

'Jake?'

No. That would put a crack in his armour, a way in, and he refused to be haunted by this woman. He would end it now. 'Carry on without me,' he said, rising to his feet. 'I have to do something. It'll just take a minute.'

Back in his office he picked up the envelope. Maybe he should take it down there. Maybe he should…

Dear God, what was it about Amy Jones? It was as if she'd invaded his mind, addled his wits. 'Call a courier, Maggie. I want this delivered right away,' he said, dropping it on his secretary's desk. Then he glanced at his watch. 'No, wait.' He'd written the address of the cottage, but she'd be at her shop for the rest of the day. 'Ring Willow Armstrong at the *Melchester Chronicle* and ask her for Miss Jones's business address. Send it there.'

'No problem.'

No. No problem. Not now.

'Any problems, Vicki?' Amy dropped her bag on her desk, along with her shopping.

'Nothing I couldn't handle. How did it go? Could you see the baby?' Vicki grinned. 'And have you bought up the entire stock of that baby boutique in the shopping mall?' she asked, taking the bags, putting them on the desk and riffling through them.

Amy laughed. 'Everything's perfect. The baby is this big,' she said, holding her thumb and finger half an inch apart. Vicki, still deep in the bags, picked out the tiniest pair of powderpuff-pink baby bootees.

'Oh, bless!'

'I know. I just went in to look but you know how it is.' Vicki emptied the bags, cooing over the precious little things until Amy made an effort to come back down to earth and called a halt, packing them away. That's when she saw the courier envelope. 'Vicki, what's this?'

'Oh, gosh. I'm sorry. That arrived just before you got back.'

Amy picked up the big square card envelope, looked at the name of the sender and with fingers that were suddenly shaking she tore it open, took out the thick white envelope inside.

She knew what it contained even before she opened it, but it was still a shock. Her joyful mood, the sweet pleasure of buying tiny clothes for the baby growing inside her evaporated like a dawn mist in August and she said a word that made Vicki blink.

'Bad news?' she asked. 'What is it? The VAT man on the warpath? Death-watch beetle in the attic?'

'Worse. It's from my baby's father.' And she ripped the contents of the envelope in two. It felt so good that she kept on doing it until the cheque was reduced to confetti. Then she picked up a fresh envelope, and after copying the sender's address from the courier slip, she scooped the shredded cheque into it. She sealed it and stamped it and tossed it in her out tray.

'Tea,' Vicki said, slowly. 'Camomile tea.' And she handed Amy a small phial of mandarin oil. 'And, in the meantime, I suggest you should rub a little of this on your pulse points. It'll make you feel better.'

She didn't want to feel better. She wanted to scream. She wanted to smash something. How dared he send her a cheque? She wanted it out of her sight. Out of her shop.

'I'll be fine, Vicki,' she said, with controlled venom. 'Just as soon as that—' she pointed to the envelope '—that *thing*…is out of my sight. Forget the tea. Take it to the post office now and send it by recorded delivery. I want to be absolutely certain that he got it.'

'Um, maybe you should wait ten minutes. Think about it. It's what you always tell me—'

'No.' She was trusting her instincts on this one. Calm thought was not the appropriate reaction. The feeling was too strong to bottle up, keep a lid on. She needed Jake to know exactly how she felt. 'Just do as I ask, Vicki. Please. Straight away.'

'Look, if you feel that strongly about it I could ask the courier to take it back with him. He was due for his lunchbreak, so I suggested the café across the courtyard.' And she blushed. 'I was going to join him if you got back in time.'

'Oh, Vicki!'

'We all have our weaknesses,' she said. 'Yours is for pink bootees. Mine is for black leather.'

'I'm not in the mood to encourage young love,' Amy warned. Then she shook her head. 'All right. Use the courier. But don't blame me if he breaks your heart. And it has to be signed for by Jacob Hallam. No one else. If I'm going to spend a fortune making a statement, I want to be sure I'm getting my money's worth.'

'You will,' she said. And grinned. 'Just you leave it to me.'

* * *

Jake frowned at the note his secretary passed to him. 'Can't you deal with it?'

'Sorry. It has to be signed for by the addressee.'

'Okay. Let's take five, gentlemen.' He got up and followed Maggie into Reception, where the courier was waiting. 'You've got something for me?'

'If you're Mr Jacob Hallam?'

'Yes.'

'Then I've got this, if you could sign for it.' He offered a pen.

Jake took it, signed for an envelope with 'Amaryllis Jones' picked out in elegant black and gold lettering on the top left-hand corner. So, she'd got the cheque. He hadn't expected such a swift response and he held the envelope for a moment; it was thick and soft and contained more than a polite 'thank you' note. As he pushed his thumb beneath the flap and ripped it open, he had a very bad feeling about it.

Jake frowned at the contents. Pink and soft. He wasn't sure what he was expecting. Nothing pink and soft, that was for sure. As he pulled it out, a handful of tiny scraps of paper fluttered about him, settling at his feet. The cheque had been shredded so thoroughly that only when Maggie began to gather up the pieces and he saw part of his signature did he realise what it was.

'What the devil…?'

Maggie handed him the pieces. 'One of two things, Jake. It wasn't enough. Or she doesn't want your money. Take your pick. But if it's the latter, I'd say you're in big trouble.'

'The question was rhetorical,' he said coldly.

Maggie had been his secretary for too long to be choked off by a chilly put-down. 'Sorry, Jake,' she said, almost kindly. 'I'm afraid trouble doesn't come in "rhe-torical". Not this kind.'

'And what kind is that?' He was just digging a bigger hole for himself, he knew, but he couldn't stop himself.

'The kind involving a woman and a cheque. Especially if she's pregnant.'

'Pregnant?' His face remained impassive, even while his gut was churning. 'What makes you think she's preg-nant?'

'Well, the pink bootees are a bit of a giveaway,' Maggie said. 'It would seem she's—you're—expecting a girl. Congratulations.'

'Bootees…' He realised what he was holding. Bootees. Blossom-pink, thistledown-soft. 'Oh…' he said. Then, 'Sugar.'

'I think, under the circumstances, a little more enthu-siasm is called for.'

'Sorry, Maggie. I can't do enthusiasm. Not for this.' He continued to stare at the bootees. They were so…so…*small*. He tried to imagine feet tiny enough to fit them. Toes… He snapped his mind back from the brink. 'She knows that. I thought the cheque would help.'

'Did you?' Maggie shook her head. 'And I thought you were quite bright, for a man. Never mind, keep try-ing. I'm sure you'll figure it out eventually.'

'You think that I'm heading for wedding bells and happy ever after?' He could read her like a book. 'Give me a break.' She said nothing, but she was thinking for England, he could see. 'Okay, what would you do? If you were me? Forgetting the white lace and promises bit,' he added quickly.

'That would depend on what I—as you—wanted.'

Maggie waited a moment. Then asked, 'What *do* you want, Jake?'

'Me? I've got everything I ever wanted.' He was successful, rich. His father would have been proud... 'I don't want this.'

Maggie gave him an old-fashioned look. 'It appears that you don't have a choice. It is yours?' She quirked an eyebrow. 'There's no doubt?' He shook his head. It was his. The only thing he could imagine worse than this situation was knowing that Amy was expecting someone else's baby. It didn't make sense, he knew, but then emotional stuff never did. 'You know, Jake, having a baby is a bit like a bacon and egg breakfast.'

He dragged his thoughts back from the golden moment when they'd made the baby. 'This should be good.'

'It takes two to make it happen,' she said, ignoring his muttered interjection. 'But while the chicken makes a contribution, the pig is totally committed. The mother of your baby can't walk away, Jake. Or pretend it isn't happening. Or pay someone else to feel the pain.' About to say more, she apparently changed her mind.

'What?'

'Nothing. At least... Well, maybe you shouldn't take the way she handled your cheque too seriously. Her hormones are probably acting up. Leave it a few weeks. Try again when everything's settled down.' Then she shrugged. 'Or you might get lucky. It might just take an extra nought.'

What did he want?

That was easy. He wanted Amy. He wanted to stop the world, rewind the tape, replay those hours they'd spent together. He wanted to breathe in the sweet scent of her skin, he wanted to wake with her in his arms, wanted to hear her whimpering softly as he took her over the edge, followed her there, briefly, to a place beyond pain. For now. He knew it was a fleeting thing. An ache that would soon pass.

Unlike fatherhood.

He didn't want to be a father. He didn't know how to be a father. Not the kind of father any baby would want. What he wanted, what he needed, was for Amy to take the money so that he could walk away with a clear conscience. Money to pay for help. Money to pay for everything.

Maggie was being over-sentimental about that. Money would do it every time. One way or the other. And Amy would take it. Eventually. She'd have no choice. But maybe sending it like that had been a mistake. It had been cold and impersonal, and she was a warm and caring woman. In her place, he realised, he would have been angry, too.

That she was angry he didn't doubt for a moment. It would take a really angry woman to reduce his cheque to such tiny shreds of paper. What the bootees meant, why she had enclosed them with the cheque, was a mystery he refused to confront. He suspected he already knew the answer. She wanted him. On his knees.

He crumpled the bootees in his hand, stuffed them out of sight in his pocket. No way.

But Maggie was right, he acknowledged belatedly. The cheque had been crass. His father would have sent a cheque. He should have thought of something less direct, something that she could have accepted without losing her dignity. A trust fund for the baby, maybe. She wouldn't, couldn't refuse that, not once she accepted that he wasn't to be turned to marshmallow by a pair of pink bootees.

He'd go down there tonight. Apologise. Check that she was keeping well. Not overdoing it. She shouldn't be on her feet all day...

Dammit, he was doing it again. Thinking about her. Worrying about her. He spat out an expletive that had once earned him a beating from...

No!

He dragged his fingers through his hair. Dear God, where had that thought come from? He'd blanked it out. Walled it up in the attic of his mind with all the other ghosts.

This was her doing. Amy, with her green eyes and gentle touch. His wall was defenceless against her. He knew, just knew, that if he wasn't very careful she would dismantle it, take it down, brick by brick, and let out all the pain. It had already begun.

Emotion was a loose cannon. Uncontrollable. And the one thing he'd always promised himself was that he would never be out of control of his life. Never again. He would get this over with. Deal with it. Finish it.

For a moment, Amy thought the courier was back. She was behind the cottage, working off her bad mood on the weeds. They would never let her down. They were predictable. They'd always be there.

She was carefully easing out a dandelion with the trowel when she heard the motorbike roaring up the lane, then slowing. Then stopping at her gate. The dandelion root snapped, leaving half still embedded in the soil.

'Damn!'

Damn, damn, damn. The day had begun so well, so joyfully; then Jake's conscience had given him a jab in the ribs and after that it had been downhill all the way.

She straightened as the leather-clad figure rounded the

side of the cottage, wondering what he'd sent her this time. A bigger cheque? Did he really believe that was what she wanted? Was he that stupid?

That scared?

The man pulled at the strap beneath the black helmet. Removed it. And her heart did a crazy flip-flop that made her feel just a little dizzy, so that she grabbed for the post of the compost bin. Not a courier this time; this time Jake had come himself. Which could be better—or much worse.

He looked tired, she thought. There were dark shadows beneath his eyes and his cheeks had a sucked-in, hollow look emphasised by the stubble of a day's dark growth of beard. He looked like a man to whom sleep was a stranger.

And the flip-flop happened again. Not just her heart this time, but her entire body responding, reaching out to him. It was a good thing that her feet were weighed down by her gardening boots, keeping her pinned to the spot long enough for her to drag her protesting heart— and hormones—back into line.

'You're the last person I expected to see,' she said.

'We need to talk, Amy. There are things we have to settle.'

Talk. Settle. Worse, then, because his voice, flat and expressionless, left her in no doubt what he wanted to discuss. He wasn't bringing his heart, but his wallet. Maybe she'd got it right when she'd suggested to Willow that money was all Jake had to offer. Not a problem when you were a millionaire more times over than you could count.

But if money was all he had to offer, he was in the wrong place. This wasn't the kind of conversation she wanted to have with the father of her child. She'd thought she'd made her feelings quite clear on that point.

Most men would have taken the hint, probably thanked their lucky stars and left it at that. Jacob Hallam wasn't most men. He didn't want to get involved but he couldn't walk away. His conscience wouldn't let him.

He was in for a bad time, she thought. And felt an unexpected twinge of pity for him.

'Have you eaten?' she asked.

'We need to talk,' he repeated. As if he'd learned the words and nothing would deflect him from his purpose.

'You can eat and talk at the same time, can't you?'

'Please don't—'

'Don't what? Make it difficult for you?' She wasn't doing that. 'I'm making it as easy as I know how, Jake. You're the one making things difficult.' She stripped off her gardening gloves. 'Have you eaten?' she repeated.

'No.'

'Then come inside and I'll get something.'

'If you insist.' His voice was firm, cold. It was the gesture that betrayed him. The tiniest lift of a hand in supplication.

He was already having a bad time.

She steeled her heart. 'No, Jake. I don't do ultimatums. You want to talk; I want to eat. Stay or go. You choose.' And she walked towards the back door, kicked off her boots and headed for the sink, forcing herself not to look back and check that he was following.

'How are you?'

How could he make the words sound so impersonal? After the way they'd been together? After such passion, such tenderness? Amy took a deep breath and made an effort to match him.

'I'm fine. I had my first scan today.'

'Scan?'

'An ultrasound scan. Just to confirm dates, check the embryo has implanted properly.' He'd like that word, she thought, scrubbing her hands at the old butler's sink. Embryo. You couldn't get much more impersonal than that when you were talking about a baby. She half turned, looked back to where he was silhouetted in the doorway, unwilling to step over the threshold. Vicki might be right about black leather, she thought. It gave a man a dangerous edge. Not that Jake needed any kind of edge to hold her attention. 'And confirm the number of embryos present,' she added, a little wickedly, just to make certain she had his.

The muscle tightening in his jaw was her only reward. 'And how many are there?'

'Does it matter?' she asked, reaching for a towel. 'It's not your problem.' Then, turning to face him as she dried her hands, 'Do multiple births run in your family?'

'How many?' he demanded, with just a hint of panic.

'Just one, Jake,' she said, her voice softening, an antidote to his sharpness. 'I was going to make an omelette. The eggs are very good. Free range...organic. One of my neighbours keeps a few chickens.'

Jake didn't want to eat. He didn't want to cosy up over supper. Didn't want to know about scans, or anything else to do with her pregnancy. He wanted to get this over with and get back to London as quickly as possible. If eating with her would speed up the process... 'An omelette will be fine.'

'Then you'd better come in.'

He propped his helmet on an old scrubbed table, unbuckled his boots, stripped off his jacket and padded into the kitchen in his socks, feeling at a disadvantage. He hadn't thought about that when he'd decided that the

Ducatti's two wheels would be a lot faster through the rush hour traffic than using a car. Right now he'd have welcomed the formality of a suit. Maybe he should have sent a lawyer.

The idea made him feel queasy. The cheque had been bad enough. He'd seen what she'd done to the cheque. His father, he realised with a sickening sense of his own inadequacy, would have followed up the cheque with a lawyer. At least he hadn't made that mistake.

She waved in the direction of a saggy old armchair. 'Shift Harry and make yourself comfortable.' It wasn't the glare from the cat in residence that kept him on his feet. Once he was sitting down he would have lost even the height advantage. Instead, he leaned against the doorjamb and watched her as she set about making their supper. The silence lengthened.

'Have you seen Willow and Mike since—' he began, then broke off awkwardly.

Amy broke an egg into a basin, stared at it for a moment, then looked up. 'Since?' she prompted. Then, 'Oh, I see. Since. Yes, Willow came over as soon as you'd gone. The poor girl was in a bit of a state. I told her not to...' She rubbed the back of her hand over her upper lip. Had it got warmer, all of a sudden? 'I told her not to worry.' She cracked another egg and watched as it oozed thickly from the shell to join the first in the basin. She hadn't noticed before that eggs had any particular smell. Not beautiful fresh, free range eggs. She picked up a third egg, cracked it on the side of the basin. Sort of oily...

'Amy?' She looked up and registered briefly that Jake was frowning. Then she was assailed by a wave of nausea and egg number three hit the floor as she turned and ran for the scullery sink.

The heaving, the throwing up, seemed to go on for ever. She hung onto the edge of the sink, vaguely aware of Jake at her back, holding her, supporting her so that she wouldn't just slither to the floor as her legs buckled beneath her.

Eventually, though, the spasms eased for long enough for her to apologise. 'It's not the cooking, I promise you,' she said, smiling weakly as she leaned shakily back against him.

He said nothing, just damped the edge of a towel, wiped it over her face, around the back of her neck, over her throat.

'Um...I hope you meant it when you said you weren't bothered about supper. I don't think I could...' For a moment she thought it was going to begin again.

'Take deep breaths through your mouth.' Jake looked down at her, at the pale damp strands of hair clinging to her cheeks and forehead. She had gone dead white before the sickness struck. She was still very pale, and in the face of her attempt at humour he felt utterly small. 'You should be lying down.' If anything happened to the baby... 'Let's get you up to bed.'

'Bed? After that? You've got to be kidding.' Then she laughed a little, just to show that she was only joking.

'Bed,' he repeated. She still looked ghastly and his heart squeezed painfully. 'Then I'll call your doctor.'

'Jake, it's nothing. Morning sickness, that's all.'

'*Morning* sickness?' What did she take him for, a fool? It was after seven in the evening. 'You know that for a fact? Has it happened before?'

'Well, no, but—'

'It could be anything. Food poisoning. Or you might have picked up some bug in the garden.'

'Rubbish.'

'That too. The compost heap is no place for a pregnant woman.' He wanted to pick her up and rush her off to hospital. 'Tell me, Amy. How can it be morning sickness when it's seven o'clock in the evening?'

'Well—' she began. Then stopped. 'I just assumed—'

'Exactly. Come on, lean on me.' About to protest that she could manage on her own two legs, that she was already feeling a lot better, she thought better of it and let him put his arm around her and help her up the stairs.

Let him take off her damp shirt. Let him help her out of her trousers. Confronted by her underwear, he hesitated, then, apparently deciding that he'd removed enough of her clothes, he held up the covers to let her slide between the sheets. Tucked her in before briefly touching her forehead with the back of his fingers.

'You're cooler,' he said, absently brushing her hair back from her face. 'You've got some colour back.'

'I feel better.'

'Is there anything you need?' Just him beside her, holding her. Holding her and their baby. That would be perfect. 'Anything I can bring you?'

'No, thanks.' Then she yawned. 'Actually, I'm a bit sleepy. That's all I need. Sleep.'

'You'll be all right if I leave you while I call the doctor?'

'Don't bother Sally. I'm fine now. Honestly.' Amy snuggled down against the lavender-scented pillow while his fingers gentled her temple. 'Absolutely great.' And she closed her eyes. She had to do that before she could bring herself to send him away. 'Can you let yourself out, Jake? Lock the door behind you?'

Jake watched her for a moment. Her colour had returned but he still wanted to hear it from a doctor, and after a moment, when he was sure she was asleep, he went downstairs. Dr Sally Maitland was listed on the fast-dial directory.

Her, 'I'll be right there,' did nothing to reassure him.

'Amy didn't want me to bother you,' he said ten minutes later, when he opened the door.

'It's no bother. She's upstairs?'

'She's drifted off to sleep. Is that a good thing?'

'The best.' She went upstairs and looked in, but didn't wake her. 'Is it her first bout of sickness?' she asked when she rejoined Jake.

'I think so. She said it hadn't happened before. But it can't be…well…just…'

'Morning sickness?'

'Well, can it? I mean it's not the morning. Nowhere near.'

'Yes, well, I'm afraid that early pregnancy nausea can strike at any time of the day.' She grimaced. 'Sometimes all day. Give her some dry toast, or a cracker when she wakes up, if she wants it. And if you can find a bottle of ginger ale about the place, she might find that helps the queasiness. I did suggest she get some in.'

'But…'

Dr Maitland's eyebrows suggested that 'but' wasn't a word she would countenance. 'You weren't thinking of leaving her alone tonight?'

His thoughts—mostly revolving around his own stupidity—weren't fit for the ears of a lady doctor. 'No,' he said, after the pause grew uncomfortably long. 'No, of course not.'

'Good.' She nodded, apparently satisfied. 'Don't hesitate to call me again if you're worried about anything.' And she headed for the door.

'That's it?'

'No point in disturbing her, Mr Hallam.' And the lines

on her harassed face arranged themselves into a smile. 'I've seen all I need. Tell her I'll give her a call in the morning.'

He went back upstairs. She was sleeping like a baby now. Her cheeks flushed with colour, her hair pale gold against the pillow. She looked so defenceless, so utterly desirable, and deep within him a siren call promised that if he just stopped fighting it, if he slipped into bed beside her and held her, everything would be fine.

He turned abruptly and took the stairs two at a time. Before he succumbed.

Downstairs, dealing with the basics, clearing up the mess, it was easier to concentrate. He didn't have any choice but to stay tonight. If at any time in the future he felt the urge to come racing down to the cottage, he'd go and lie down in a darkened room until the feeling passed.

The next time he checked on her, she stirred. 'How're you feeling?'

She focused on him from the depths of her pillow. Blinked. Frowned. 'Jake? You're still here? I thought you'd be long gone.'

'Of course I'm still here,' he snapped. 'Did you think I'd walk out and leave you?' He could have phrased that more carefully. What else would she think? 'I came here to talk to you. And your doctor assumed I'd be staying.'

'You called Sally?'

'I thought you were ill. Having never been in this situation before, I wasn't aware that morning sickness doesn't necessarily mean *morning* sickness.'

'Confusing, isn't it? And you didn't get any supper, either.'

'I'm not helpless, Amy. I don't need waiting on. Quite

the reverse in fact. I'll get something for you. She suggested dry toast,' he added.

'Yummy,' she said, unenthusiastically.

'That's a thumbs-down for dry toast, is it?' She made a thumbs-down gesture. 'What would you like?'

Amy eased herself up into a sitting position and knew exactly what she wanted. Jake had arrived at her cottage, a leather-clad, macho man of the world, determined to put an end to this relationship, certain that it was simply a matter of haggling over how much it would cost him. The idiot. Now he was hovering anxiously in her bedroom doorway, trapped by his own conscience and clearly wishing he was anywhere else.

There was something utterly endearing, she thought, about a man totally out of his depth. That look of helplessness was irresistible.

Controlling an errant sigh, she resisted the urge to tell him what she wanted most in the world. She'd promised herself that she wouldn't do a thing that would give him cause to accuse her of entrapment. Not a thing. But keeping him at arm's length was proving more difficult than she had anticipated—considering she'd just been very, very sick. So she concentrated instead on food. That was a surprise, too.

'I'd like a sandwich.'

'I can handle that.'

'Plain wholemeal bread, no butter,' she began. 'Pile on the lettuce—not cold from the fridge, get it from the garden. You'll find some I've brought on under a cloche.'

'Amy, it's the middle of the night,' he protested.

'Is it?' She glanced at the window. 'Don't worry, you'll find a torch by the back door.'

'Oh, right. No problem, then,' he said, with only the faintest suggestion of irony.

'Then cover the lettuce thickly with mayonnaise—'

'Mayonnaise?' This time he did look concerned. 'You're quite sure about that?'

'Mayonnaise,' she repeated firmly, 'topped with a layer of sliced dill pickle.' And she smiled. 'That would be perfect.'

Terrific. Morning sickness, closely followed by food fads. All in one evening. He should have listened to the voice of reason and stayed in London, Jake decided as he toured the pitch black garden looking for lettuce. Except Amy would have been alone when she'd been sick.

There would have been no one to make sure she was all right. No one to call the doctor. Okay, so he'd panicked unnecessarily. But what if it had been something more serious? He wouldn't have been here.

He didn't want to be here.

But as he constructed her nightmare sandwich it occurred to him that there was finally something that he could do to help, something he could organise that would allow him to keep a safe distance between them and at the same time ease his nagging conscience.

CHAPTER THREE

THIRD MONTH. All your baby's organs are now formed and most are beginning to function. Movements develop, such as wriggling toes and pursing lips. You will have probably gained about one kilogram in weight. It's time to visit the dentist.

THERE was a woman sitting on the small bench in her porch, Amy realised as she got home. Not anyone she knew.

'Hello,' she said. 'Can I help you?'

'Miss Amaryllis Jones?'

'I'm Amy Jones,' she said, getting out her key and hoping this wouldn't take long. Her feet ached and she was desperate for a cup of tea.

'Dorothy Fuller.' The comfortably built middle-aged woman offered her hand. She had nice eyes, a warm smile. A motherly look. She also had a much-used suit-case. 'How d'you do?'

Amy found such formality from a casual caller on her doorstep slightly unnerving. 'Are you selling some-thing?' she asked, glancing at the case.

'What?' Then Dorothy Fuller laughed. 'Oh, no. The agency sent me.'

'What agency? What for?' Amy asked, deciding that it might save time if she doubled up on questions.

'The Garland Agency. I've been engaged as your housekeeper.'

'Housekeeper?' A housekeeper with a suitcase. The suitcase was beginning to seriously bother her, but she slid the key into the lock and opened the door. She'd been rushed off her feet all day, the bus had been late and crowded, and if she didn't sit down some time soon she was going to crumple up on the floor. 'I think there must be some mistake.' She glanced up at the small cottage, as if to underline the fact that anyone with half a brain could see she didn't need a housekeeper. 'Are you sure you're in the right place?' she asked. 'This is Upper Haughton. People sometimes confuse it with Lower Haughton—'

'No confusion, Miss Jones. I know my Uppers from my Lowers,' she said, unoffended by the doubt cast on her navigational skills. 'Miss Garland called me into the office to brief me herself and she said I was to give you this.' She handed Amy an envelope and while she was opening it picked up her suitcase and walked in. 'Now, I could do with a cup of tea and I expect you could, too. So why don't you go and put your feet up and I'll see to it?'

'But...' But Mrs Fuller had taken herself off to find the kitchen, leaving Amy to deal with the envelope. She was beginning to take a quite irrational dislike to envelopes. Or rather their contents. This, a short note from Jake, did nothing to improve her opinion of them.

Amy,
Mrs Dorothy Fuller, I am reliably assured, will look after you like a mother hen. She's from the Garland Agency; they know her well and totally guarantee her probity. I've put her on my company payroll so you needn't concern yourself with the financial implications, and meanwhile I'd feel happier knowing there

was someone on hand to take care of you.

Please don't tear her up into little chunks and send her back by courier.

Jake.

Jake. He arrived on her doorstep, did the ministering angel bit and then walked away. She'd heard nothing from him for what seemed like for ever. Then, when she'd managed to convince herself that he'd taken her at her word and gone, he did this.

She wanted to hug him, and yell at him, and tell him he was a fool. Mostly she wanted to weep, because Jake thought he could distance himself this way, pay someone else to do his worrying for him.

He was wrong. Dead wrong. He stayed or he went. She'd given him the choice, no strings attached. She wasn't offering any in-between, half-way options. He couldn't choose 'go', then seek to salve a troublesome conscience like this. No way.

Mrs Fuller appeared with a tea tray set for two and placed it on a low table in front of the sofa. 'Sit down, dear. I think we need to have a little chat about how this is going to work. I'll tell you what I can do; you tell me how you'd like me to fit around you. I don't want to disturb your routine, or get in your way.'

'You won't do that, Mrs Fuller.' She wouldn't disturb her because, no matter how sweet she was, how trustworthy, she wasn't staying.

But Jake was right about one thing. Returning the lady minced up in a shepherd's pie was not the answer. She'd done 'angry' when she'd got his cheque.

She'd have to find some other way to make her point.

*   *   *

Jake regarded the envelope with misgivings. It had been a couple of weeks since he'd engaged Mrs Fuller. He'd checked with the agency and been assured that she'd arrived safely in Upper Haughton and had reported back to say that she was enjoying her new assignment. It all sounded too good to be true.

After the cheque incident he had been sure that Amy's reaction to the arrival of a housekeeper would be to throw a hissy fit. He was relying on Dorothy Fuller to make herself indispensable in double-quick time. She'd come highly praised as a woman who could win around even the most testy and uncooperative of women to the joys of live-in help. Maybe she'd done just that. Maybe this was simply a note from Amy to thank him for his thoughtfulness.

Somehow he doubted it, which was why he was looking at the envelope as if it was an unexploded bomb.

'It's just a letter,' Maggie said impatiently. 'Give it to me. I'll open it.' She twitched it out of his hands, slit the envelope and held up a neatly typed missive for his inspection. 'Not a bloodstain in sight, see.' She scanned the contents, then began to chuckle.

'I didn't invite you to read it.' Then, 'What does she say?'

'Basically, thank you. And that's she very happy with the arrangement.'

'Why do I suspect that's not all?' He clicked his fingers irritably, held his hand out for the letter.

Maggie ignored him. '"Dear Jake,"' she read—which was a good start, better than he could have hoped for under the circumstances. '"This is just a quick note to let you know that Dorothy Fuller arrived safely last week. I'm sorry I haven't written sooner to thank you, but I'm decorating the spare room at the moment—"'

'Decorating?' He had a sickening vision of Amy standing on a wobbly stepladder, struggling with wallpaper. He waved his hand. 'Go on.'

'''I'm decorating the spare room at the moment, which is why I didn't have room for her at the cottage. I've installed her, temporarily, at the farm down the lane—'''

He rose to his feet. 'She's done what?'

'She's put her up in the farm down the lane—'

'No! That undermines the whole purpose of the exercise. She needs someone with her—'

'''…down the lane, where they do bed and breakfast in the summer. Don't worry, Jake, this won't cost you any extra. Good help is always hard to get, so they were happy to take her in return for some cooking and cleaning, and my little house wouldn't keep her busy for more than a day a week. She is frighteningly efficient…'''

Jake spun around, stared out of the window where London was laid out beneath his feet. At university he had designed a telecommunications program, dropped out to start his own company and built a fortune with a single-mindedness that should have warned him he would never escape his genetic history.

Every day he took decisions involving millions of pounds without raising a sweat.

But this woman…this woman could bring him to his knees with half a dozen words.

'Keep going,' he said curtly.

Maggie cleared her throat. '''She seems to be enjoying herself helping out with the guests, and after all, she'd get terribly bored on her own here all day.'''

'Bored? Why would she get bored? She can read a book, knit a shawl for the baby…' He stopped. He didn't want to think about the baby.

'"Also,"' Maggie continued, once she was certain he had finished, '"and I know you won't mind this, I've asked her to keep an eye on Mrs Cook opposite. She broke her leg last week and she's finding life a bit difficult at the moment. She can't afford to pay for help herself, so you'll be glad to know that she's finding Mrs Fuller an absolute treasure."' Maggie looked up expectantly.

He raised a hand in helpless gesture of surrender. 'I'm absolutely delighted that she's an absolute treasure,' he said. 'Thrilled to bits.'

'"She's been taking care of the twins on the corner, too, after school, and helping out at the old folk's lunch club at the church…"' He groaned, let his head fall into his hand. '"…and although I haven't seen much of her myself, she assured me yesterday, when I passed her on my way home from work and met her taking old Mr Blacklock to see Sally at evening surgery, that she really enjoys working in the village. Well, it is a lovely place to live. I'm not sure how long you'll let me keep her, Jake, but what with Social Services being so stretched—"'

'Enough!' He turned and glared at Maggie, who was doing her best not to laugh out loud. It was plainly something of an effort. 'Laugh and you'll be looking for another job,' he warned.

'I'll get on to the agency and have them call Mrs Fuller off, shall I?' she spluttered, not in the least bit intimidated.

'Call her off? Have you forgotten Mrs Cook? And what will the twins do without her?'

'Oh, come on, Jake. Surely you don't believe any of this nonsense? She's just trying to wind you up.'

'Then she's succeeding. Dear God, all I want to do is make life a little easier for her, but no. She's up a step-

ladder papering the ceiling and the housekeeper I'm paying for is now playing Good Samaritan to the entire pop-
ulation of Upper Haughton.' He got up. 'Cancel my
appointments. I'm going to settle this once and for all.'

'But I thought the whole point was to avoid—' He
turned to glare at her and Maggie quickly shook her
head. 'Nothing, Jake. Just…take care.'

'It's a bit late for that. If I'd "taken care" none of
this would be happening.'

'I meant on the road. You seem a bit distracted.'

Jake walked into the cobbled courtyard of the old coach-
ing inn in Maybridge that Mike Armstrong had turned
into a complex of shops and business accommodation
for local craftsmen and tradespeople. Mike's own workshop, where he designed and made fine furniture, oc-
cupied one side of the yard.

Amy's shop was opposite. The narrow frontage,
painted in black, had the name 'Amaryllis Jones' picked
out in gold lettering. It was a small but exquisite em-
porium, filled with exotic aromatherapy oils, beautiful
scented candles, fine soaps. Small, but very busy.

He sat outside the corner coffee shop that, taking advantage of the sun, had overflowed into the courtyard
and watched for a while, considering what it would take
to persuade her to accept his help. With care, extra
hands, financial support, whatever. What it would take
to make her see that in refusing his help she was denying
her baby all the special things his money could buy.

Maybe he wouldn't use that argument. Complaining
that she was denying him a chance to assuage his feelings of guilt probably wouldn't impress her that much.

And maybe she really didn't need his help. She had
a charming home and a thriving business. No one, he

noticed, left the shop without one of her distinctive black and gold carrier bags. It must be hard work, though. She'd be on her feet all day. Wouldn't she get swollen ankles? Shouldn't she be resting? Or was that dated nonsense? What he knew about pregnant women could be written on the back of a postage stamp.

Maybe it was time to stop trying to second guess her and simply ask what she wanted. And hope it was something in his power to give.

He paid for his coffee, crossed the courtyard and pushed open the door. There was a delicate chime to announce him, crystals turned in the draught, catching the sunlight, and the air was full of the warm, heavy scent of roses. Then Amy appeared in the doorway from the rear.

Black and gold.

She was dressed in unrelieved black. Her hair pale gold. It was the same every time he saw her. The jolt. The longing for something that seemed unreachable, on the far side of an uncrossable void.

'Jake.' It was the same every time she said his name. Like a ride in a high-speed lift going to the stars.

'Amy.' For a moment they just stood there, looking at one another.

'How...unexpected.'

'I doubt that.' She didn't deny it. 'I had your letter,' he said, when the silence became unbearable. 'I was concerned to read that you were decorating.' His voice was clipped and abrupt. A long way from what he was feeling. 'What are you doing?'

Her shrug was infinitesimal. 'Having fun. I've finally settled on the exact shade for the nursery ceiling.' Her smile was all behind her eyes. A secret smile. As if dwelling on anticipated joy. 'That gorgeous translucent blue the sky turns just as the stars start to come out. All I need now is to find a match so that I can get it mixed.' And then her smile became public, less intimate. 'Look, do you mind if we talk and walk at the same time?' she asked. 'I've got an appointment at the dentist.'

'You've got toothache?' He wanted to kiss it better. Her mouth, her eyes, every inch of her—

'No, it's just a check-up,' she assured him, interrupting his mental tour of her body. 'I'm three months pregnant.'

'Three months?'

'Nearly.'

'It doesn't seem that long.'

And for a dangerous moment they were both reliving the moment.

'Pregnant women need to look after their teeth,' Amy said quickly, reaching for her bag.

'Oh.' Make that a very small postage stamp. Then, because he'd never seen a car at the cottage. 'Do you drive?' He held the door for her. 'I'll drive you there if you like.'

She shook her head. 'No, thanks; I'd be early. Besides, walking is good for me. Vicki,' she called back, 'I'm off now. I'll be about an hour.' Then, 'It's this way. If you're coming.' And she set off in the direction of the town centre without waiting for his answer.

'How are you?' he asked, falling beside her. 'Still being sick?'

'Oh, yes. Seven o'clock on the dot. You can set your clock by me, but the ginger ale is helping and now I know what to expect it's not so bad.'

'You look well.' Blooming. Wasn't that what they said about pregnant women? It was true.

She gave him a green sideways glance. 'That's just a

polite way of saying I'm putting on weight,' she said, then laughed. 'Don't look so tragic. I'm having a baby. I'm supposed to be putting on weight.'

'You don't mind?'

'I'm happy to be pregnant. I can put up with a little inconvenience to my waistline.'

'Are you? Really happy?' He stopped, frowned. She looked it, but he didn't understand. She was on her own so why would she want this? 'It's not just the weight. It's the sickness, the teeth. Everything. I'd do all that for you if I could.'

'I believe you. You'd do anything but be a father.'

'I'm so sorry, Amy. Really sorry.'

She reached out, took his hand. 'Hey, I was there, too. I'm happy, honestly. I'm ready for this. A baby, motherhood. It's the right time for me.'

'Is it? I suppose women are different.'

'Not that different.' Then, not giving him time to respond, she moved on, his hand still in hers, 'I suppose you've come to tell me off about Mrs Fuller?'

'Maggie—my secretary—thought you were just trying to wind me up. Were you?'

'Winding you up?'

'She assumed that you were making up all that stuff about the village.'

'Why would I want to do that?'

The space between her eyes creased slightly in a frown that he suspected was not quite as innocent as it looked. She knew what she was doing. Not that it mattered. She could wind him up simply by breathing—a fact he thought safer to keep to himself.

'Why indeed?' he replied evenly, playing along. He hadn't doubted a word of it, not for a moment. It sounded all too plausible. He was sure that if she put her mind to it she'd have Dorothy Fuller jumping through hoops at the village gymkhana. 'Of course, she doesn't know you—' He'd been going to say, as well as I do, but it occurred to him that while her body was imprinted indelibly upon his mind, he knew very little else about this woman who was apparently delighted to be bearing his child. 'I hoped you'd be taking things easy. Is decorating wise?'

'I'm not doing much. Just painting the nursery. Maybe a little stencilling. Stars, do you think?'

'On the ceiling?' She'd said she was going to paint the ceiling. 'I've painted ceilings. If you think it isn't hard work, you're in for a nasty shock.' He could picture the scene all too easily. And the picture gave him the shivers. 'Should you be stretching, bending, climbing ladders?' She didn't answer. 'Will you let me send someone to help with that at least?'

'Would you?' For just a moment he thought that he was getting somewhere. Then she said, 'I promised Mike I'd help paint the village hall this summer, and an extra pair of hands would be—'

'Forget it.'

Then he glanced at her and realised she was grinning. Definitely winding him up this time. 'No decorator?' she asked.

'Not one you can twist round your little finger the way you have Mrs Fuller.'

'Spoilsport.'

'Just a fast learner.'

'I was afraid you might be.' She stopped at an antiques shop as something caught her attention. 'Will you look at that?'

He looked. The centrepiece of the window display was an age-darkened wooden cradle, one of the rockers worn where countless women had rested a foot to gentle a restless baby to sleep.

It would look absolutely right in Amy's cottage, and for a moment he hovered on the brink of offering to buy it for her. Something warned him not to. 'It looks really old,' he said. 'Elizabethan? Stuart?'

Her hand rested lightly against the window, as if she was communing with all the babies that had lain within the safety of the crib, with all the mothers who had rocked it. 'That's real history.' Her voice was cobweb-soft. 'Can you imagine, Jake? Some woman centuries ago telling her husband that she was having his child. And her husband searching out just the right tree, cutting it, shaping it...' She didn't look at him. Didn't expect an answer. And after a moment she moved on.

He glanced at her, half expecting her eyes to be filled with tears. His own throat ached unfamiliarly. He swallowed. 'You didn't answer my question back there,' he said, abruptly changing the subject. 'Do you drive? I haven't ever seen a car at the cottage.'

She looked up at him. 'That's because I haven't got one.'

'Oh, no, that's right. Mike said you use a broomstick.' Maybe Mike was right. He had this odd feeling that he'd been bewitched. Today he was supposed to be meeting a business contact for lunch. Reviewing progress on a new contract. He'd never intended to be here, walking Amy to the dentist, her fingers laced through his. He knew she'd be better off without him. But how to convince her? 'Tricky with a pram, though. How do you do business?'

'On the phone, the internet, by mail order.'

'Mail order?'

'It's a big part of the business. I have a lady who

comes in two mornings a week just to deal with that. She used to do it at the cottage, but I need the room now so I've rented extra space here which means we can expand.'

He was impressed. But still concerned about transport. 'Shopping?' he pressed. 'How do you manage that?'

'Just for one. Not a problem. But I'm thinking of getting it delivered. Did you know you can shop online through the supermarket?'

'I had heard,' he said wryly.

'Of course. You're in that business yourself.' He nodded once. 'As for myself, I'm perfectly happy to use the bus service.'

'Still tricky with a pram,' he pointed out, trying not to think about her struggling on and off buses as the months passed and she got bigger, as it took more effort. At the end of a long day on her feet. She needed a car—

'I shan't be investing in one of those large, coach-built jobs that require a uniformed nanny at the helm— and,' she said, before he could interrupt, 'I'm warning you now, before you do something really stupid like having a Volvo estate delivered to my door with a pink bow—'

She could read his mind apparently. Well, nearly. He hadn't thought about what model estate he'd buy her. As for the colour of the ribbon, he was almost certain that it was too soon to determine the sex of her baby.

'Not pink.' She wasn't the only one capable of doing a little winding up. 'It'd be a blue bow.'

'Blue, pink—believe me, it would be a complete waste of time. I've never learned how to drive.' As he bit back, with difficulty, a suggestion that now would be a good time, she stopped. 'I go in here.'

'Here?'

'This is the dental surgery.' She retrieved her hand, touched his cheek briefly. 'Do stop worrying about me, Jake. I'll be fine.'

And before he realised what was happening he was standing alone on the pavement, with the door shut in his face. Again.

Well, not this time. He pushed the door open and was confronted by a receptionist with a smile that was a dazzling advertisement for her employer.

'Can I help you?'

He doubted it. He was beginning to believe he was beyond help. 'No,' he said. 'I'm in the wrong place.'

'If you're nervous, sir, we can offer...' He didn't wait to hear what she could offer for his nerves. He was beginning to think it would take more than a tranquilliser to get him through this.

Amy, in the waiting room, heard Jake follow her into the surgery. Then retreat in some confusion. The easier she made it for him to leave, the less inclined he seemed to be to go, she thought.

'Miss Jones.' She wanted so much to go after him. Ask him why he kept coming back. 'Miss Jones, we're ready for you now.'

'What? Oh, right.' She got up and followed the receptionist through to the surgery. It didn't matter why he kept coming back, so long as he did it because he cared. The last thing she wanted in her baby's life was a daddy who was just going through the motions.

And what was all that macho stuff about a blue bow? He wanted a son? Why would a man who'd made it very clear he didn't want a baby under any circumstances care one way or the other about what sex it was?

*   *   *

Jake walked away from the dental surgery, but he'd stopped trying to fool himself that this was over. Amy might keep telling him to go, but he had responsibilities whether he wanted them or not, the kind he couldn't walk away from.

He knew all about responsibilities. Every day he held the lives of the men and women who worked for him in the palm of his hand. They relied on him, his vision, his energy, his drive, to ensure that they could pay the mortgage, put food on the table, take their families on holiday.

Maybe that was the answer. If he could deal with this situation dispassionately, treat it as just another project needing his close attention, he wouldn't get bogged down in emotion.

What he needed was information. He was floundering in a woman's world that he knew nothing about and was tired of feeling at a disadvantage. Passing a bookshop, he stopped and turned in. It was time to buy himself a little equality.

The assistant was eager to help. 'You're going to be a father?' she asked, when he enquired about books on pregnancy. She didn't wait for answer, but went on, 'Is it your first baby?'

'Er, yes.'

'How lovely,' she said, picking out titles that she thought he might find useful. 'When is it due?'

He realised he hadn't asked Amy when she was expecting their baby. That was appalling. It was the very least he could have, should have done. Realising the woman was waiting for an answer, he did a little mental arithmetic. 'December,' he said.

December. And he thought about heating. He'd seen a stack of logs at the cottage. She couldn't cope with log fires, she'd need central heating, a drier for the baby's clothes...

'You modern men are so involved, so different from when I had my children.' She smiled. 'You're going to be at the birth, I suppose?'

'What?' No! Of course he wouldn't be at the birth. That was unthinkable. But if not him, who? Who'd hold Amy's hand while she went through the long hours of labour?

Hold her hand and what else? There must be more to it than that. He had some vague idea that Mike had gone to antenatal classes with Willow, learned about the whole process, about breathing through the pain...

'Oh, dear. You look quite pale just thinking about it. Just be grateful you're a man, simply an onlooker.' Then she patted his arm sympathetically. 'Don't worry, you'll be fine.'

Fine. He escaped with the books. Sure, he'd be fine, but what about Amy? Would she be fine? There wasn't enough money in the world to pay for someone else to be with her, in his place, while his son was born.

He returned to the courtyard café to wait for Amy to return. He ordered a mineral water, then opened one of the books. A month-by-month description of the development of the baby. A month-by-month description of what the mother might expect as her body adapted to the needs of her growing infant.

He stared at the photograph of a developing foetus for a moment, only two inches long and already wriggling his toes. He snapped the book shut. He was getting far too involved, getting much too close. He stood up, put his hand in his pocket for change and his fingers closed over the bootees.

* * *

Vicki looked up as Amy walked through the shop. Followed her into the office. 'How was it?'

Amy dropped her bag on her desk. 'Fine. All that working out with the toothbrush paid off,' she said, putting the conversation firmly in the teeth corner, although they both knew that Vicki hadn't been talking about her visit to the dentist. 'Everything's perfect.'

Everything was perfect. Running like clockwork. Exactly right. She was having a baby and absolutely delighted.

So why had her heart taken a little dip when she'd come out of the surgery and Jake hadn't been pacing the footpath, waiting for her? Hadn't been sitting in the coffee shop when she got back? She'd seen him there earlier, watching the comings and goings, no doubt assessing her turnover, checking out her ability to support his child.

He wanted to talk, he'd said. About transport? And business? That was all? There was a reprise of the heart-sink as she realised that his mind was still firmly fixed on finance.

'He came back,' Vicki said, as if reading her mind. 'He'd been to the bookshop on the corner and he sat over there with a pile of books about pregnancy.'

Amy found a smile from somewhere. 'You're making that up.'

'No.' Vicki grinned. 'My aunt works at the bookshop so I phoned and asked her what he'd bought...'

Books on pregnancy? The smile became less forced. 'You asked your aunt to betray a professional confidence? That's appalling...'

'You don't want to know?' Vicki shrugged, turned away to tidy a shelf. '*Growing a Baby,*' she murmured, half under her breath as she began to replenish the stock. *'The First Nine Months…'*

Back at his desk, Jake opened his electronic notepad and began to work up a strategy for dealing, at a safe distance, with Amy's pregnancy. The trick would be to do as much as he could for her without getting personally involved.

No more touching.

He could still feel her fingers, cool against his palm, as she'd taken his hand, held it while they'd walked to the dentist. A faint citrus scent still clung to his fingers. Not orange. Something sweeter, lighter, that made him feel better just to breathe it in. Or maybe it was simply the scent of her skin.

He realised he was holding his hands up to his face and snatched them away.

Definitely no more hand-holding.

What he needed was a plan. Normally he'd call a team meeting, ask for ideas, assign tasks, monitor results and make the big decisions.

His team so far consisted of Dorothy Fuller, and Amy had swiftly neutralised her. Well, maybe. He'd talk to Dorothy, make sure she kept a close, if discreet, eye on her charge and reported back to him on a regular basis. Dr Sally Maitland might yet prove to be an ally. He'd go and see her, talk to her. And Willow had been through all this so recently that she could keep him up to speed with what Amy would need by way of support.

And then there was the decorating. He wouldn't be sending a man in an overall with stepladders and instructions to do whatever the lady wanted. If he did that he'd find himself paying to have half the housing stock of the village redecorated. There had to be another way.

In the meantime, he'd offer her something she couldn't get anywhere else. A skill not so readily available. That 'All I need now is to find a match so that I can get it mixed' was a start. Seeing the perfect colour in the sky was a long way from getting it in a paint tin. It was time for the decorator he'd employed on the penthouse to prove that she could do more than be creative with taupe.

CHAPTER FOUR

FOURTH MONTH. At the end of this month, you may feel your baby move for the first time. With luck the sickness will have tailed off. The baby's fingernails are beginning to develop and he's nearly as long as your hand.

JAKE couldn't believe it. Fingernails. His baby, as yet no bigger than his thumb, was growing fingernails.

He had been so sure that once he knew exactly what was happening, how the baby grew, what to expect from Amy in the way of reaction at each stage of pregnancy, he'd be able to manage things, control them. Regain control of his life.

He'd been fooling himself.

This was like being a kid again. A kid no one cared about, no one took any notice of, until he raged at the world, smashing the things people did care about. They'd taken notice then, but not in any way he'd hoped for.

He stared at the photographs charting the baby's development and felt...vulnerable. He hadn't felt so powerless, so helpless since he was ten years old.

He wasn't in control; the baby was in charge here. All he could do was offer security and even that was subject to Amy's co-operation.

And she wasn't co-operating.

He'd been so impatient and excited over the last few

71

weeks, waiting for the decorator to come up with ideas, a reason to drop in at the cottage…

Now the folder had arrived, complete with shade charts, fabric samples, totally co-ordinated colour schemes that were the very last word in a designer nursery. It lay on the table beside him and mocked him.

Amy would hate it. Hate the phoniness of it. Hate the distance it put between head and heart. He picked up the folder and flung it at a vase. Even before it toppled, smashed against the polished blonde wood floor of the penthouse, he knew that breaking things wasn't going to help. It hadn't helped when he was ten years old and a quarter of a century on nothing had changed.

Weeds, weeds, weeds. The weather was warm and wet and everywhere weeds were growing faster than she could pull them out of the ground, and a plague of slugs was devouring her plants as quickly as she could plant them.

Amy subsided onto the damp earth, and as she surveyed the bare stalks of her runner bean plants she howled with frustration. Which was ridiculous. The battle with nature was a yearly event. Nothing to get worked up about. But this year it had all been so much more effort. She was so tired. For the first time since her pregnancy was confirmed, hot tears cascaded down her cheeks.

Damn Jake with his sexy smile, his totally perfect body and the haunted look in his eyes that cried out to her—Love me. She shouldn't have listened to his eyes. She should have listened to his words.

He'd warned her. She'd thought she could handle it. She could handle anything. But this time she was wrong. He'd bought baby books and she'd been sure that meant he cared, but it hadn't meant a thing because he hadn't come back. And a great racking sob wrenched at her body.

Her next-door neighbour, glancing over the fence to see what all the fuss was about, called Willow.

'It's not like her. It's just a few beans, for heaven's sake, and it happens every year.'

'Just leave her with me,' Willow said as soon as she arrived, ushering the old lady out of the garden.

'She shouldn't be struggling with the garden in her condition. And you needn't look at me like that, Willow Armstrong. I didn't get to be seventy-eight without being able to tell when a woman's expecting a baby. Where's the father when he's needed for something useful? That's what I'd like to know.'

'I'll make her a cup of tea—'

'Tea? If I was asked my opinion, which I won't be, I could tell you that it'll take more than tea to get her through what's ahead of her...'

Jake was picking up the broken pottery when the phone rang. 'Jake Hallam,' he said.

'Don't you Jake Hallam me,' came back at him in a fierce whisper. 'Where have you been?'

'Nowhere...working...'

'There are more important things in the world than making money. It's time you put your clever mind to sorting out the mess you've made—'

'Willow? What's the matter? What's happened?'

'I've just found Amy sitting in her vegetable garden in tears—no, breaking her heart. And I don't think it's over a few beans, do you?'

The question was clearly rhetorical, since she didn't wait for an answer before hanging up.

'Beans?' he repeated. Then frowned. 'Tears? According to all the books she shouldn't be tearful for another month.' Grabbing his car keys and heading for the door, it occurred to him that this was no time to be complaining that Amy wasn't sticking to the schedule laid out in all the baby books he'd read in the past couple weeks.

Tears were good. In fact tears were great. They were the first sign of weakness she'd shown. Maybe now she'd be ready to listen to reason. And he went back for the decorator's folder.

Willow opened the front door as he walked up the path, her finger to her lips. 'Amy's asleep in the back garden. She's tired, Jake. She shouldn't be gardening.'

'You think I don't know that? I sent her a housekeeper to ease the load. Where is she this afternoon?'

'It's Sunday. Even the most peripatetic of housekeepers usually get Sunday afternoon off.' Yes, of course they did. Stupid of him. Willow put her hand on his arm. 'I'm sorry. I'm sure you're doing all that you feel you're able to.'

Damned with faint praise, he said, 'Do you want to show me what upset her in the first place?'

'I've got to get back to my own family. Just take a look at the vegetable plot and you'll see the problem. And bear in mind that while it might not seem much to you, when your hormones are up the creek without a compass it doesn't take a lot to set you off.'

'I suppose not. Willow?' She paused. 'Thanks for calling me.'

'Who else is there? She has no family.'

'None?'

'None that I've ever heard her speak of.'

They had that in common, then. 'Willow?' She turned in the gate. 'That estate you drive, would you recommend it? For a mother?' She came back and gave him a silent hug, as if she understood how hard this was for him. She didn't, but under the circumstances it was kind of her to try. He watched her for a moment as she hurried back to Mike and her own baby, then he walked around the side of the house.

Amy was asleep on a garden lounger laid out in an arbour shaded by thick, sweetly scented honeysuckle. Her cat, stretched out on the ground beside her, looked up at his approach.

He bent, rubbed Harry's ears gently for a moment, watching the slow rise and fall of her breast as she slept. Then he realised that if she woke and saw him standing over her she'd probably get the fright of her life, so he tore himself away to examine the damage to the vegetable garden.

Maybe, he decided, looking at the row of bare stalks, it wasn't hormones that had turned on the waterworks. If he'd spent as much backbreaking effort in growing his own vegetables, he might just weep at the decimation to the crop.

He looked around. The weeds were getting ahead of the flowers, he realised. The grass needed cutting. He'd have to start getting tough about this, insist that she let him get some help for her, at least for the heavy stuff.

Then he'd have to find someone who could be relied on not to be subverted to the good of the village while Amy carried on in her own sweet way. He was no longer fooling himself that this was going to be simple, but she needed to be convinced that she couldn't do it all.

He glanced back at her. She was still sleeping. He

could sit and watch her or do something useful. Watching her was a deeply appealing idea.

Useful, he suspected, would be wiser. And, sleeping, she couldn't stop him from helping.

Amy stirred, lay for a moment listening to the sound of a hoe chopping into the soil, the occasional clink of a small stone. 'Willow?' she half turned, opened her eyes. 'You shouldn't be...'

Not Willow. Jake.

Stripped to the waist, working in her garden.

Lean, hard, his finely muscled body gleaming in the late-afternoon sun as he bent to his task, he looked wonderful, better than the dreams that had haunted her sleep.

Each time he went away hurt more. Each time he managed to stay away a little longer. Six weeks this time, and she thought she'd die for want of him. And now he was back, working in her garden. Jake himself, hoe in hand, clearing the weeds from the vegetable garden. Not someone he'd paid to do it.

Domesticity of the kind on which dreams were built.

Castles in the air.

She swung her legs off the lounger and sat up abruptly. The world spun and in an instant he was at her side, pushing her head down between her knees.

'Don't sit up so quickly or you'll faint,' he said, taking her hand as if concerned that she might fall.

'I know that,' she said irritably, pulling her hand free. 'What are you doing here?'

'Willow rang me. She thought you could do with a little help in the garden.'

'She shouldn't have done that.'

'No, Amy. *You* should have called me.'

'And asked for help out of working hours? Isn't it difficult getting agency people on a Sunday?'

He straightened. 'Absolutely impossible,' he said. 'It's a good job I had nothing more exciting planned. Can I get you anything? Tea? Something cold? A sandwich?'

'Why does everyone think I need an endless supply of tea?' she demanded crabbily. Then held up her hand. 'That question doesn't require an answer. I can take a hint.'

His hand dropped to her shoulder as she began to rise. 'Stay there. I'm the hired help for today.'

'That can't be cost effective. How much is your time worth by the hour?'

'A lot more than the average jobbing gardener, so you'd better make the most of it.'

His smile, for all its self-mockery, was infectious. While she didn't know what to make of his concern, couldn't fathom his motives for responding to Willow's SOS, she decided that it didn't matter. He was here and for the moment that was enough.

'You'll find some camomile and honey teabags by the kettle. And there are some ginger biscuits in the tin.'

Once that had been settled, he quickly took his hand away. Her shoulder immediately felt cold; she shouldn't have capitulated quite so quickly, she thought. Then was cross with herself. No tricks. No lures. No feminine wiles to keep him at her side. He'd know and he'd despise her for it. But not as much as she'd despise herself.

So she stayed where she was, feet up, eyes closed, until she heard the clink of the tray as he put it down on the ground beside her before reaching for his shirt, hanging on a nearby branch.

'How's the decorating going?' he said, as he turned and saw her watching him.

'It isn't,' she said, taking the mug he stooped to pass to her. 'I still haven't found the exact colour match for the ceiling.' She shrugged. 'To be more exact, I haven't had time to look. But there's no hurry.'

'Are you sure about that? How much ladder-climbing time do you think you've got left? Six, eight weeks? And that's ignoring the fact that you shouldn't be climbing ladders at all.'

'Six weeks will be plenty of time.'

'Assuming you find your colour straight away. Fortunately, I know a talented decorator.' There was a folder lying on the tray beneath a plate of biscuits. He picked up the plate, offered her a biscuit, then handed her the folder. It bore the name of a well-known interior design consultant. 'She's used her database to try and find exactly what you're looking for.'

'You've commissioned a decorator to design my baby's nursery?' she asked.

She didn't easily betray her feelings. She'd learned early in life that emotion, visible expressions of it, embarrassed people. Jake Hallam was making it difficult to keep up the calm façade.

Delight that he'd taken the trouble warred with the knowledge that he'd employed someone to do the hard work for him. He didn't want the commitment, the responsibility of fatherhood, any of the effort. But he just couldn't resist the fun parts.

'Without asking you first? As if I would.' His innocent grin didn't fool her for a minute. 'I just asked her to come up with some colours. Anything else is purely wishful thinking on her part.'

'And shrimps can whistle.'

'She'll keep going until you get exactly what you want. Check them out and let me know. There's no hurry,' he said, echoing her own words. None at all. The longer it took, the bigger she'd be and, hopefully, the more amenable to offers of help. 'But personally I think the navy stripes are very classy.'

His smile didn't disguise his tension as he waited for her reaction, certain that she wouldn't be able to resist taking a peek.

'Thanks,' she said, smiling right back. 'I'll bear that in mind.' And she put the folder down on the far side of the lounger.

He sipped the herb tea. Pulled a face. Tried another tack. 'Why don't you drive?' he asked.

The cup wobbled in her hand. This was too much. 'Does it matter?' she asked.

'You'll need to drive. You might be able to manage your business without transport, but you won't be able to combine a full-time career and motherhood without a car. Ask Willow. She'll tell you.'

Amy took a slow deep breath. This was something she didn't want to talk about. 'This is none of your business, Jake. I don't know why you're here. You don't have to be.'

'So you keep telling me. Do you want me to walk away, is that it? Do you really believe I could be that uninterested in the welfare of my baby?'

His baby? That sounded just a mite possessive for a man who'd tried to buy his way out of responsibility.

'She's not yours, not in any way that matters. Your interest, or lack of it, is no concern of mine.'

'Have you lost your licence?' he persisted.

He would think that. Why couldn't he just accept that some people didn't want to drive? 'Do you mean lost as in mislaid? Dropped somewhere? Can't find?' she enquired politely. No answer. Of course not. They both knew that if that were the case she would simply apply for a replacement. 'No, Jake. I haven't lost my licence. I've never had a licence to lose. Only a learner's licence and that was a waste of time because I never did learn to drive.'

'Then it's time you did.'

Breathe. Smile. Breathe. 'It's not something I've ever wanted to do.'

'So why did you apply for a provisional licence?'

'Because it's what you do on your seventeenth birthday. Because you can. It doesn't mean anything.' Other people managed without cars. She'd just need to be totally organised. She was good at that. 'Holding a driving licence isn't compulsory, Jake,' she said in a tone that made it quite clear that the subject was closed.

He listened to the words, heard the cool, dismissive tone and knew she was faking it. He couldn't say why. There was nothing to betray her. But it seemed that he was tuned in to every nuance, every gesture. Had been since the moment he set eyes on her.

That cool, totally controlled front Miss Amaryllis Jones put on for the world he already knew was just that—a front. He'd been there when she was hot, burning with passion and totally out of control, and he knew there was a lot more to the lady than an unsettling look that left you feeling psychologically exposed, emotionally naked.

Maybe that kind of intuitive conduit flowed both ways because, try and hide it as she might, he was feeling her pain as if it were his own. Not driving wasn't a choice she'd made. She didn't drive because she was afraid, and impulsively he reached out for her hand, held it.

'Do you want to tell me about it?'

'Jake.' Her voice warned him that he was trespassing.

Intuition urged him to press her, because this was important.

'I might be able to help.'

'I don't need help.' She tugged her hand free from his grasp, swung her feet to the ground and stood up. 'Heavens,' she said, dragging her fingers through her hair and looking about her, anywhere but at him. 'Haven't you done a lot of weeding?'

Jake unwound himself slowly from the grass, but kept his distance, respecting the touch-me-not force field that was holding her together. He should be grateful for it, he knew. It was all that was keeping him from taking her in his arms and promising that whatever had happened in the past, whatever was so bad that she couldn't face talking about it, he was here to make sure that nothing could ever hurt her again.

Empty, meaningless words. He wouldn't promise what he couldn't deliver. He knew how it felt to be on the receiving end of hollow words.

'If you've got any more bean plants, I'll put them in for you,' he offered. 'Before I go.' Practical help was something he could do. Then, catching her doubtful expression, he said, 'I haven't always lived in a penthouse.'

'I know. Willow told me that you'd been in care. Fostered. When she was telling me that you were going to be Ben's godfather.' When he didn't respond to this prompt, she let it go. 'It's getting late to plant out beans.'

'They'll soon catch up.'

She shrugged. 'There are a few plants left. If you really want to do it, they're in the greenhouse.'

'I'll get them. If you've got an empty washing up liquid bottle I could find a use for that, too. And a pair of scissors.' He'd got her full attention now, the remembered horrors sliding back into the past as she tilted her head to one side with a smile that tucked up the corners of her mouth and made him long to reach out for her, pull her close, kiss her.

If he hadn't found out about the baby so precipitately it was probable that he would be making hot, sweet love to her now, blissfully ignorant of the time-fused secret about to blow up in his face.

Was that his problem? A childish pet because this dalliance hadn't had a chance to run its course, had ended before it had begun? Before he'd grown tired of it? Was that the reason for his restless need to keep coming here? Because he still wanted her with an ache that increased rather than diminished, his desire apparently inflamed by the knowledge that she was carrying his child?

One part of him wanted to lie with her, hold her, be part of this miracle. The other part understood the impossibility of it. That was the part he should be listening to.

'Scissors?' Amy repeated, in disbelief.

He dragged himself back to the present, the sweetness of the garden, a blackbird singing somewhere nearby. 'Pinking shears would be even better.'

'This,' she said, 'I have to see.'

An hour later, with Amy's precious plants protected by serrated circles of plastic—a trick he'd learned from the practical, down-to-earth woman who'd fostered him— Jake opened the fridge door and regarded the contents.

'What are you doing?'

'Thinking about supper. You haven't got much in. You should be making an effort to eat properly for the baby's sake, even if you are feeling sick. Is this cheese pasteurised?' He glanced back at her. 'You should only be eating pasteurised cheese. You do know that?'

'Yes, Jake,' she replied solemnly. 'I do know that. But thanks for the interest.'

'And plenty of green vegetables.'

'Tell me, did you learn this from *The First Nine Months*, or did it come from *Growing a Baby?*' Jake felt the heat rise to his face. Could she read his mind? Was Mike right...? She scooped up the cat, who was stropping her ankles, and said, 'Vicki—my assistant—has an aunt who works in the local bookshop.'

'I would have thought the books one bought were privileged information.'

'You'd have thought so. But then, you haven't met Vicki.'

'Actually it was from *Father-to-Be*,' he confessed. 'Would you like to read it? It's full of really useful stuff about—'

'I'm sure your need is greater than mine, Jake. I'm already up to speed on all the really useful stuff. And, since I'm not an invalid, I'm allowed out after eight o'clock. Why don't we go down to the pub and have someone else slave over a hot stove for us? It's what I'd planned to do this evening.'

'By yourself?' he demanded, then realised just how possessive that sounded. Jealousy had no place in this relationship. Oh, yeah? Not much. An amused and scathing voice inside his head taunted him. He ruthlessly suppressed it. 'If I'm in the way, just say.'

'On the contrary, a man who'll pick up a hoe without being asked is always welcome,' she said, ignoring a question he wished he'd never asked. 'Just remember that it's your choice that you're here. I didn't ask you to come.'

'It's a good thing someone did.' Then, 'I'm sorry. You're a grown woman, quite entitled to go into a pub on your own.'

'Yes, Jake,' she said. 'I am.' Then, 'This is a very friendly village. Everyone knows everyone else. And most of their business,' she added thoughtfully, her look steady. 'Will that bother you?' She meant that most people would know that she was pregnant, and if he was with her they'd take it for granted that he was the father of her child. The man who wasn't offering a quick trip up the aisle. 'We could go somewhere else if you'd prefer?'

Run away? Hide? He was damned if he would. Let the world think what it wanted; he knew he was trying to do his best for Amy and the baby. It wasn't his fault that she refused to co-operate.

'The pub will be fine,' he said.

They walked across the green, keeping a clear foot of space between them by unspoken consent. As if they both knew that touching wouldn't be a good idea. It was the christening all over again, and while his mind was keeping them apart, his body was plotting all kinds of ways to get close. Then, as they entered the pub, Amy stopped briefly, frowned.

'What is it? What's the matter?'

'Nothing.' He wasn't convinced but she shook her head. 'Really, I'm fine.' She headed for the bar. 'What do you want to eat?'

'Sit down, I'll see to it.'

'You're the hired help.'

'I'll charge it to expenses. What would you like?'

'Whatever pasta dish they have on the menu.' Then she grinned. 'Just be sure to check that the cheese is pasteurised.' Before he could answer, she added, 'And I'll have a ginger ale.'

'You're feeling queasy?' He felt an immediate and answering nausea.

'No. I like ginger ale. And while you're there you can catch up with Dorothy.'

'Dorothy?'

'Dorothy Fuller, the housekeeper you're paying to keep an eye on me. That's her, playing darts. Golly, she's good, isn't she? The pub could do with her on their team.'

'They can have her; she'll be staying for a while. You might be able to manage without her at the moment, but you'll need her eventually.' He crossed to the bar, ordered food, trying to ignore the unsettling feeling that he was on the edge of quicksand and that whichever way he moved he was going down.

He carried the glasses back to the table, sat beside Amy in the window seat. She glanced at his own drink. 'You're drinking ginger ale, too? I hope you're not getting sympathetic nausea?'

'I'm driving,' he said glibly. 'Tell me what happened just now,' he said. 'When we arrived. And don't say nothing. I know something did.'

'I felt the baby move. At least, I think I did.' She laid her hand against her waist very gently. 'It was so faint, a tiny flutter, like a butterfly... Oh, yes!' She reached for his hand and put it beneath hers so that he could feel it, too. 'There!'

It was so small that he wasn't sure he'd felt it. He didn't much care. Just to touch her, to feel the warmth of her body as he laid his hand against her waist was enough. Then she smiled again. The tiny flutter could have been his imagination. Her face told him that it wasn't.

'Should we be here?' he asked, his voice struggling through emotional treacle. 'Maybe you should have your feet up…'

'What did it say in all those books you've been reading, father-to-be?' He shrugged helplessly. 'All those books and you still don't know?'

He looked up, realised that she was laughing at him and took his hand away.

'You're not taking this seriously.'

'You're wrong about that. I've never been more serious about anything in my life.'

'Really? So have you decided where you're going to have the baby?' Practicalities. Stick to the practicalities. 'Is there a good nursing home around here? Should I book you into somewhere private? In London, if you like?'

'Yes. And no.' Before he could interrupt, she said, 'Yes, I've decided where I'm having the baby. And, no, the private maternity hospital won't be necessary. I'm having her at home.'

'At home? Are you kidding?' His voice rose and the people at the next table stopped talking, turned round and gave him a suspicious look. Amy smiled, reassuring them. 'That's positively Dickensian,' he said, when he'd regained her attention. 'No one has babies at home any more. Suppose something goes wrong? It'll be December. Suppose it's snowing and an ambulance can't get to you? No,' he said, 'I won't allow it.'

That appeared to amuse her. 'I think you'll find that you don't have any say in the matter.'

'Dammit—' He stopped as a young girl brought cutlery to the table, waiting impatiently for her to go. 'Dammit, Amy—'

'Yes?'

'I can't stand this.' She waited. 'I can't stand being excluded. This is my baby, too. I want him to have my name. I want—' He stopped. He no longer knew what he wanted.

She put her hand over his. 'If you want your name on her birth certificate, Jake, you just have to come along to the register office with me. But don't think it gives you any say in where she's born.' There was a hiatus while the waitress brought their food, checked that they had everything they needed, took Jake's order for another drink.

'Home births are risky, aren't they?'

'No, but don't take my word for it. Check it out in one of those books you're so keen on quoting.'

'I will.'

Amy picked up a fork and began to eat. Jake had earned his place on the birth certificate because of his very real concern for her and her baby, even if he would prefer to help at one person removed and believed that money could take the place of personal commitment.

More than that would require a sea change in his attitude.

'Tell me what you've been doing since I last saw you,' she asked, deliberately changing the subject. 'What do you do when you're not working?'

For a moment she thought he would persist, but after a moment he shrugged. 'I'm always working. I don't have time for anything else.'

'Not even your family? You don't see your mother? Willow told me—'

'Willow knows nothing about my mother. I have no

mother,' he said flatly. 'No family. None that I want to know. There's just Lucy.'

'The famous Aunt Lucy?' she said, letting the rest go. One day he'd tell her. When he was ready. 'She's fostered dozens of children through the years, hasn't she? She must be a pretty amazing person.'

'I suppose she is.'

'Have you told her about the baby?' He shook his head. 'Maybe you should.'

'Oh, yes, I should certainly do that. The trouble is I know what she'll say.'

Amy laughed. 'You're a bit old to be sent to bed without any supper.'

'Not too old to be made to feel as if I should be,' he said ruefully. 'She's a real old-fashioned lady with real old-fashioned standards.'

'I could come with you, if you like. I'll swear it was all my fault.'

Amy's eyes sparkled at his discomfort. Lucy would love her, he knew. As he did. His heart seemed to pause, wait for his head to catch up. His head didn't appear to be in any hurry, but it would get there eventually.

Love was a meaningless word, too easy to say, too hard to live up to. He'd excised it from his vocabulary.

'Thanks for the offer, Amy, but she wouldn't believe you. And if I took you to meet her when I told her about the baby she'd assume we were getting married.' He placed his fork very carefully on his plate. 'Maybe that's the answer.'

She waited a moment, not quite sure if she'd heard right. 'Excuse me?'

That he wouldn't marry was the one thing he had been certain of. But this was different. There would be none of that moonlight and roses pretence. It would simply be a practical arrangement. 'It would make sense. That way I could look after you, both of you, properly.' He'd have rights, too. Rights to insist that Amy took sensible precautions, had her baby somewhere with every facility.

'Was that a proposal, Jake?'

He was slow to look up, face her. 'I'm offering you security. That's all.'

'Your name and your bank book?'

'It's all I have to give. Take it or leave it,' he said, more harshly than he'd intended.

'Er…I'll leave it, thanks.' One step forward, two steps back, Amy thought as she lifted a fork and began to eat, slowly and carefully, aware that he was watching her with that completely baffled expression that she found so endearing.

'What do you want, Amy?'

You. All of you. Body and soul. Unless she was prepared to settle for his wallet, this was not the moment to weaken.

'Nothing. I told you. Forget it.'

'I've tried. I can't forget it.'

'But you want to. You can't face the responsibility of caring for a fragile life, something that relies on you entirely, is that it?' He didn't answer. 'Always having to be there? In person? Always putting her first? Afraid of being needed and not being able to deliver? That, like your mother, you'll run out when the going gets tough?'

'If that's what you want to think.' Jake didn't disabuse her. It was marginally less painful than the truth. And at least he wasn't pretending, playing a role he was unfitted for.

'I just wanted you to know that I understand. That I'd rather you just walked away than try and do what you believe to be your duty. It would be easier.'

'You think so? If you want me to go, Amy, make it easy. Take the money.'

'I'm truly sorry, Jake. I can't do that.' She turned away, staring up at the blackboard behind the bar. After a long moment, she cleared her throat and said, 'Offer me strawberry gateau and I might be tempted.'

CHAPTER FIVE

FIFTH MONTH. Your baby is moving distinctly now, and you will begin to look noticeably pregnant. Some women become tetchy and irritable and occasionally weepy at this time. It's time to think about booking antenatal classes.

JAKE abandoned a spreadsheet and opened the book of babies' names that he'd bought at lunchtime, flicking through it, picking out names at random. Mark? James? James Hallam sounded good. James Jones did not. He didn't like it one bit.

George. That was a strong, solid name. George Hallam. George Hallam Jones. He frowned. It was the Jones bit that was the problem. Marriage was the only way to fix it, but Amy hadn't taken to that idea. Well, she wanted a lot more than he could give.

They'd walked back to the cottage but she hadn't asked him in, had simply turned to him, kissed his cheek and said goodnight. When the door had shut between them he hadn't felt relief. He didn't know what he'd felt. Only that he hadn't liked it. In fact he'd hated it. Hated it so much that he'd spent the last month chasing up a business lead that any other time he'd have left to someone else, just to keep himself from thinking about how much he hated it.

Yet he'd still found himself wandering around fashionable baby stores, marvelling at how small the clothes were. Touching the pink bootees in his pocket. Buying books filled with names that no one in their right mind would ever inflict on an innocent baby. He'd still found time to organise a car for her.

Maggie put her head around the office door. 'The car's arrived. Do you want to go down and check it over, or shall I get someone else to run the driver back to the garage?'

He got to his feet. 'I'll do it myself. I want to get the feel of it before I take Amy out in it.'

'You?' She laughed. 'You're going to teach her to drive?'

'You've got a problem with that?' he enquired irritably. Maggie's scarcely veiled amusement at his dilemma was beginning to wear dangerously thin.

'None whatever. It's a great move if you want to guarantee she'll never speak to you again. Is that the plan?'

It was one answer. But not one that would convince his nagging inner voice, or make sleep any easier. Sleep was very hard to come by. He only had to close his eyes to be taken on a slow motion rerun of his night with Amy.

'If I book a course of lessons for her she'll just cancel them, and I can't think of any other way to ensure she gets behind the wheel and stays there.' He wasn't totally convinced he could persuade her to do this, but he had to try. 'I won't be back today.'

She paused in the doorway. 'Why don't you make that the rest of the week? Your body is coming into the office but your mind seems to be elsewhere.'

'Don't be ridiculous. I can't just waltz off in the middle of—'

'Jake,' she said gently, stopping him. 'If you fell under a bus tomorrow would the company cease to function?' He stopped. Frowned. He was the company. His brains, his name…but, no, it wouldn't cease to function. 'We might all run around like headless chickens for a week or two, but no one is completely indispensable. Not even a genius like you.' When he didn't answer, Maggie said, still gently, 'You run it. Not the other way round. Take a couple of days off and sort out your minor domestic crisis—'

'It's not…' he began, then stopped.

'A crisis?'

'Minor.'

She smiled. 'Okay. Make that three days. You've got your cellphone. If there's a panic you can be in the office in an hour.'

'An hour?'

'Sorry,' she said innocently. 'I assumed you'd be staying in Upper Haughton. My mistake.'

'No, mine. But maybe you're right. This needs my full attention. Reschedule my appointments for the rest of the week. Once I've got Amy properly organised, I can forget it.'

'Right,' she said. She didn't sound convinced.

'Amy, it's Jake.'

Amy opened her mouth, swallowed, pressed the little cellphone closer to her ear. It had seemed like for ever since he'd come racing down to the cottage at Willow's insistence and she was beginning to think that he'd taken her at her word. And forgotten her. She wasn't finding it that easy to forget him. He haunted her mind in a way she could never have imagined. He was the last thing on her mind as she drifted off to sleep, her first thought when she woke. Alone.

That was increasingly hard.

And each time he took her by surprise she found it a little more difficult to maintain a cool, low-key reaction. Just the sound of his voice was enough to send her heart flying up to her throat, making it extraordinarily difficult to simply say hello. A warning of just how painful it would be if he did finally take her advice to walk away and 'forget it'.

She'd bear it; she'd survive. She'd survived worse. But she was beginning to wish she'd said yes when he'd asked her to marry him...

Dear Lord, what was she thinking?

She took a deep breath, remembered that she was a fully functioning human being who didn't need a prop to support her. A partner was something else—a man at her side who would acknowledge her as unique, precious, equal. She didn't want a man who was chained to her by duty because in the heat of passion they had made a baby.

'Amy? Are you there?'

'Sorry, Jake,' she said, and cleared her throat. 'A customer had a query.' And when she was back in control, her heart behaving itself, could trust her voice, she continued, 'Now, what can I do for you?'

'For me?' He sounded as if the idea of her doing anything for him was an alien concept. 'Nothing. I was simply checking to make sure you'd booked antenatal classes.'

Not, How are you? How's my baby?

'What?' she asked, aspirating crisply.

'Antenatal classes. According to my book you should be thinking about them now.'

'Really?' So that was how he was handling it now. By the book. 'Well, thank you for letting me know. I'll be sure and get right on to it. If that's all, I'm very busy—'

'No…I thought we might have dinner tonight.'

'Oh? Did you?' She wasn't going to play the I'm busy—it's too short notice games, but she wasn't about to sound as if he'd just made all her dreams come true. Even if he had.

There was a pause while he apparently waited for her to fall in line with his thought processes. Then, when he realised she wasn't going to oblige, he said, 'Would you have dinner with me this evening, Amy? If you're not doing anything else? I realise it's short notice and that you have a life—'

He caught on quickly and she rewarded him with a laugh. 'Tuesdays through Saturdays at the shop, paperwork in the evening and pregnant to boot. A life? Not so's you'd notice.'

'Is that a yes?' he enquired, not falling into the trap of taking her acceptance for granted. He was very quick about some things.

'I'd love to have dinner with you.'

'Thank you.' There was another pause and it occurred to her that there was more to this call than antenatal classes. She didn't leap in to fill the gap, though, leaving him to say what was on his mind.

'Have you settled on the colour for the nursery ceiling yet?' Jake asked, finally breaking the silence.

The nursery ceiling? That wasn't what she'd expected. She hadn't had time to give it much thought and she'd hardly expected him to be worrying about it.

'Not yet. Maybe you'd like to help me choose?' she offered.

'I'll be glad to. What time do you close? I'll pick you up at the shop and we could go to the local DIY store.'

'Not tonight. I have to dash to the supermarket after we shut and I don't know how long I'll be. I should be home by sixty-thirty. I'll see you there—'

'Don't dash,' he said. 'Make a list and I'll do your shopping for you. Then you won't have to carry it on the bus.'

'Oh, sure. I can just see you at the business end of a shopping trolley, racing down the aisles hunting down the bogofs.'

'Hunting down the *what*?'

'Confess, Jake. You haven't been in a supermarket in years.'

'On the contrary, I still occasionally take a week off to help out Aunt Lucy in the Eight 'til Late Shop she refuses to give up despite all my efforts to install her in an all mod cons bungalow in Bournemouth.'

'You should make an effort to associate with more amenable women.'

'Give me a clue,' he said, ignoring her interjection. 'Is it a breakfast cereal?'

'Bogof simply stands for "buy one, get one free", Jake. As you'd know if you'd been in a supermarket any time in the last twelve months.'

'Really? Well, I'll be sure to look out for them. Unless you're addicted to shopping trolleys? In which case I'll come and help you push.'

'Waltzing around the aisles of a supermarket in tandem sounds dangerously domestic for a man with a commitment phobia.'

'Supermarket aisles hold no terrors for the well-organised bachelor. Not unless they've started doing cut-price weddings in the deli.'

'You're impossible, do you know that?'

'Impossibility is what I do best, sweetheart. Make the list. Now. And don't forget the broccoli—'

'Don't call me sweetheart!'

Jake left his car, swiftly crossed the cobbled courtyard and pushed open the shop door. A young woman behind the counter packing one of Amy's distinctive black and gold carriers looked up.

'I won't keep you, sir,' she began, then, as she recognised him, stopped uncertainly. He put a finger to his lips.

Amy was in the office. She was standing, her hand to her back for support, the light from the window streaming around her lighting her up like a halo. She looked pregnant, he realised with a jolt. The flat plane of her abdomen was now a gentle curve where her baby was growing. Their baby. His hand, with the phone, dropped to his side.

'Jake? Are you still there?' she said. He clicked off the cellphone. 'Damn, I've lost the signal.'

'I've come for the list. Is it ready yet?'

He saw her look at the phone in her hand, frown. Then she turned and saw him. And the frown dissolved into a smile before she could arrange her features into that coolly ironic glance that she did so well. The way her eyes lit up made him feel ten feet tall.

He crossed to her, took her hand, kissed her cheek. Her skin was like peach satin, her scent something elusive, floral, intoxicating. She was the perfect picture of womanhood, everything that a man might dream of. If he was capable of dreaming.

'You should be sitting down every chance you get,' he said, releasing her while he was still capable of letting her go. 'And you should be wearing sensible shoes.'

She looked down at the high heels she was wearing.

'I know. I've got some with me but I've been putting off wearing them for as long as I can. I'm getting fat, and there's no escape from that, but I'm trying to put off looking frumpy for as long as possible—'

'You couldn't look frumpy if you tried.' He led her across to the chair, waited for her to sit down and, when she did, he bent and took off her shoes. 'You're beautiful,' he said, looking up at her. 'You'll always be beautiful.'

She leaned forward, laid a hand briefly against his cheek. 'And you, flatterer, are welcome any time.'

'I hoped you'd say that.' He found the little flat pumps beneath her desk and held them out for her to slip her feet into. 'I've taken a few days off.'

'Oh? And what do you intend to do with them?'

'Sort you out so that I can stop worrying about you.'

'I don't need sorting out. And I've told you that you don't need to worry.'

'I need a little help with that. Take the money, or the help I send you—'

'I let you weed my garden,' she protested.

'Yes, well. That's why I'm here. Your generosity was noted, considered, and now I'm acting on my conclusions. You won't let me pay for help, but you'll allow me to do it myself.'

She smiled. 'You're very smart.'

'No, if I was smart, I wouldn't be in this situation. But I'm a quick learner. Which is why I've taken a little paternity leave in order to decorate the nursery.'

'Jake…' Amy's throat was momentarily constricted by emotional overload, and instead she simply put out her hand, took his, held it.

'I thought I could get a room at the farm that does bed and breakfast,' he prompted.

'It's the school holidays. They're fully booked.'

'Maybe the pub, then, or failing that I'm sure Mike and Willow would let me use their spare room.'

'I've got a spare room.'

'Then why isn't Dorothy Fuller in it? You said she couldn't stay because you were decorating—'

'I know, but I've been too busy to make a start whereas if you were in it you could fall out of bed and pick up a paintbrush. If you're serious?'

'Try me. Jot down what you need from the supermarket and I'll go and stock up. Then I'll drive you home.' She reached for a notepad and he watched as she listed half a dozen items. She used a fountain pen and had exquisite handwriting. He wasn't a bit surprised. He took the note, but didn't immediately leave. 'Have you thought about getting someone in to cover for you?' he asked. 'While you're on maternity leave? Maybe I could help?'

'That's very kind, Jake. How much do you know about aromatherapy?' Her face was deadpan, but her eyes sparkled wickedly.

'I meant I could help you find someone.'

'Oh, I see. Well, actually Vicki's taking charge. She knows as much as I do about this business. Her sister's going to start coming in part time next week. She'll be here full time while I'm having the baby and we'll see how it goes after that. Does that answer your question?'

'Amy, I could do with some help in here!' Vicki called.

'I'll be right there.' She grinned as she offered her hand for him to pull her up out of the chair. 'Trust me, Jake. I know what's important.'

She stood in front of him. Even in flat shoes she was uncommonly tall for a woman. Uncommonly beautiful. Uncommonly desirable. That he desired her with an urgency that left him utterly exposed, defenceless, was painfully evident as his body responded to her like a moth to a flame.

'No, you don't, Amy,' he said, angry with himself, with the weakness that kept bringing him back to her. 'If you knew what was important you wouldn't have torn up my cheque.'

She lifted his hand to her cheek, rubbed her face against it. 'I thought I was making some progress with you, Jake,' she said, before letting him go. 'I have customers waiting.'

She left him standing alone in her office as she went to help Vicki with the customers. He could hear her voice, gentle, warm as she explained how to use lavender oil in a neck massage to help someone sleep. Considered how it would feel to have Amy's fingers kneading at the painful knots of tension in his own neck, her hands moving slowly over his shoulders. Considered how it would be to do the same for her. Falling asleep together. Waking together. For the rest of their lives.

For a moment the thought lingered enticingly, then he snatched up the shopping list. 'I'll pick you up here when you close,' he said, easing through the sudden rush of customers.

At the doorway, he looked back. No matter what happened to either of them, he realised in a sudden rush of understanding, they would be forever linked. As if she heard his thought, she looked up suddenly. And smiled.

Amy tried to concentrate but her mind kept straying to Jake and what he thought he was doing here. Money hadn't worked, so he'd changed tactics. Thought practical help would do the job, get him off the guilt hook.

It was a start, she told herself. The first step to emotional responsibility.

It was what she'd been waiting for.

It wasn't enough.

She wanted him the way he'd been that first time they'd met. Not thinking at all. Responding, reacting to a need he was still refusing to admit to, the very human need to love and be loved.

For once she doubted her own ability to understand, see what was happening, ease the path for someone confused, in pain. Maybe because this was too close, too personal. Maybe she had Jake Hallam all wrong.

'It's gone half past, Vicki. Lock up, will you?'

'You don't want me to lock your man out, do you?'

Amy glanced up, saw Jake heading across the courtyard. 'He's no one's man but his own,' she said.

'"No man is an island, entire of it self", Amy. Come December your baby is going to make sure of that. And he's yours for tonight. Better make the most of it.'

'Yes,' she said. And then smiled at the thought. 'I suppose I had.'

Jake pushed open the door. 'Ready?' he asked.

'She's ready,' Vicki told him. 'Go and have some fun, the pair of you.'

'I've just got to—'

'You've "got to" nothing, Amy. I can handle locking up.'

Amy smiled. 'You could handle it all. I'm just grateful you haven't had any ideas of opening your own shop.'

'With "Vicki Johnson" above the door? It doesn't have quite the same ring as "Amaryllis Jones" does it? That's a name to turn heads. I wish my mother had been that imaginative.' She picked up Amy's jacket and handed it to her. 'Off you go. And I don't want to see you here before ten o'clock tomorrow morning.' Vicki grinned at Jake. 'I'm holding you personally responsible for making sure she has a lie-in.'

'I'll do my best,' he replied gravely, ushering Amy through the door. He offered his arm and after the briefest hesitation she looped hers through it. 'It's a lovely evening. I thought we might eat down by the river.'

He clicked the remote on his key ring as they approached a top of the range family estate car, the rear of which was stacked with supermarket bags. She raised her eyebrows. 'How long are you thinking of staying?'

'They're just a few bogofs,' he explained, with a totally straight face. 'Disposable nappies. Cotton wool. Baby shampoo. And I made you a member of their special club for mothers-to-be—'

'You're kidding!'

'No. It's great. You get magazines and stuff. A card that gives you special discounts—'

Amy covered her mouth with her fingers. 'You stood at the customer service desk and filled in an application form to become a member of the Bunny Club?'

'Oh, you already know about it?'

She swallowed, hard. 'Mmm. I was going to join, I just—' He waited. She just wished she'd been there. 'I just hadn't got around to it yet. Thank you, Jake. It was very thoughtful of you.'

He held open the passenger door and waited for her to get in. And that was when she stopped noticing the shopping and thought about the car. It was a world away from the slinky sports car or the terrifyingly fast motorcycle he usually drove.

Solid, safe, utterly reliable. It failed to fit any image she had of Jake Hallam. Willow, however, who just happened to be a young mother with a busy full-time job, had exactly the same model. A coincidence? She didn't think so.

'You have a new car?' she asked.

'It was delivered today. Do you like it?'

A loaded question. 'It doesn't suit you.'

'I have different cars for different roles. This is my country car. Built to deal with muddy lanes, pot holes and with bags of room for shopping, carrying paint, that sort of thing.'

'Horse feathers. If you'd picked yourself out a carry-all workhorse, it would have been a Jeep or a Range Rover or something equally big and masculine.' She paused. 'And it would have been black. Not bright yellow.'

'Actuarial statistics prove that yellow cars are involved in fewer accidents,' he said, straight-faced.

'I can believe it. You could see this monster coming from half a mile away in the foulest weather.'

'Yes, well, would you care to get in now, so we can get back to the cottage before the ice cream melts?'

Whatever game he thought he was playing, on this occasion he was doomed to disappointment, so she climbed aboard and permitted herself to be distracted.

'Ice cream? What kind of ice cream?' she enquired.

'Praline and cream.'

'Then there's no need to worry.' And she grinned. 'It's never going to get as far as the fridge.'

'Is this wise?' Jake asked.

She was sitting at the kitchen table, the wickedly expensive tub of ice cream open in front of her.

'Trust me. It's the best idea you've had all day.'

'You're not going to eat it all?'

'Of course not. That'd be greedy.' She waved a spoon

at the chair opposite and waited. 'It's beginning to melt,' she warned him, when he hesitated. Jake shrugged, pulled out the chair and lowered himself into it. Then, and only then, did she scoop up a spoonful of the ice cream and put it in her mouth. 'This,' she said, 'is almost the only way to eat ice cream. Try it.'

She refilled the spoon and offered it to him.

'Almost?' he said, the word escaping before he could stop it.

He knew that this was a dangerous game to be playing with a woman he desired beyond reason, a woman with whom a simple sexual dalliance was now out of the question. When every gesture, every word was loaded. When one careless move would have the situation spiralling out of control in a situation that could only end messily with pain and misery all round.

He did not do commitment, he reminded himself. It was something he was having to do with increasing frequency. The fact that he was here, sitting at Amy's kitchen table, warned him how far he had drifted from that simple philosophy.

The ice cream was running over the edge of the spoon, trickling down her fingers, onto her wrist, and he decided that she was wrong. There were lots of ways to eat ice cream and his imagination was fast fowarding through them all.

He wanted to lick it from her fingers, from the hollows of her elbow, her shoulder, her breasts—

'Almost,' she confirmed. Teasing, vivid, her eyes never faltered, keeping him her captive, heating him up from the inside so that the ice cream would sizzle as it slid down his throat. 'I've heard that naked with a blindfold is absolutely sensational—'

He erupted from the chair. She could read his mind.

Or maybe, on reflection, it didn't take extra-sensory perception to anticipate where his mind was headed. He fetched two dishes from the dresser, and another spoon, and silently scooped out the contents of the tub, sharing it between them.

Amy said nothing, but her brows twitched slightly. He was glad she found it funny because he had a joke waiting up his sleeve. The difference being, he was in deadly earnest.

'Finished?' he asked, when she'd licked the spoon clean. Slowly. Thoroughly. Tormentingly. 'I'll put the shopping away while you change.'

'There's no rush, is there?' She glanced at her watch. 'It's only just gone six o'clock. It's incredible to be home so early.'

'I'm sure I can think of some way to fill the time.'

Amy had been intent on provoking Jake. Pushing him, hoping to break through his self-imposed restraint. He'd kissed her cheek and her entire body had responded, demanding more. Jake, though, was a man in total control of himself.

Very nearly in control. He clearly found ice cream very tempting.

But now, although his words suggested dalliance, their tone did not. Without warning he'd turned the tables, taken control.

'Jake…' she began uncertainly, aware that she should apologise for turning up the heat. But, then again, not actually wanting to.

'You've got fifteen minutes,' he said.

Jake headed towards the river, but instead of turning off for the restaurant he'd mentioned he carried on for a while, explaining that he had something he had to do first.

'Why are we stopping here?' Amy asked as he pulled into a recently closed aeroclub with a small airfield. Jake got out of the car and went to the rear of the vehicle, bending over it. 'What's wrong?' She climbed out and followed him as he walked around to the front. He straightened and she saw the learner plate fixed to the car.

'Into the driving seat with you.' She stared at him in disbelief. 'You haven't got long to get this right, Amy. In a couple of months you'll be too big to sit comfortably behind the wheel, so let's not waste time.'

'You're the one wasting his time,' she said, furious with him, scared, because he looked so determined. And frighteningly close to tears. She bit her lip. 'I told you I don't want to do this.'

'If you want to eat tonight, if you don't want to walk home, you're going to have to,' he said, his face expressionless, offering her no clue to his thoughts. 'You can do it naked if you think it will be more fun,' he offered 'But I'd advise against the blindfold.'

She turned and looked around, as much to hide her blushes as in any earnest search for a way out of this. Besides, the entrance to the airfield was a good half-mile away. And farmland stretched around them, barren of human habitation. It didn't matter. The car had a phone; she'd call a cab. She climbed in, picked up the receiver. There was no dialling tone.

'In your own time,' Jake said, apparently convinced that he had her beat. He didn't know her. She slid out of the seat. Half a mile was nothing, she told herself as she headed for the exit. 'It's five miles to the nearest phone,' he called after her. 'Give or take a couple of hundred yards.' She made no indication that she had heard. 'That's an hour and a half at a brisk walk.' She'd gone less than twenty yards when she heard the car start, and he drew up beside her, matching the car's speed to her brisk walking pace. 'Dammit, you need transport, Amy.'

She didn't stop, didn't look at him. 'I realise you live in a different world from the rest of us,' she said furiously, 'but you'll be amazed to learn that hundreds of thousands of women, with and without babies, manage every day of their lives without the luxury of their own car.'

'Not out of choice.'

'This *is* my choice,' she said, finally coming to a halt.

'No, it isn't. You're afraid. That's not making a choice, it's giving in, capitulating to something you can't control.'

He sounded so matter-of-fact. As if this was something that could be handled by directly confronting it. Did he think she hadn't tried? She'd lost count of the number of driving courses she'd booked. And then cancelled. Couldn't begin to remember the times, encouraged by friends, when she'd got behind the wheel of a car, reached for the key…fallen apart.

'Please,' she begged. 'Don't do this.'

He turned off the engine, got out of the car, leaned back against the door, arms folded, going nowhere. 'Tell me about it.'

She glanced at him. 'I know what you're up to, Jake.'

'I'm just trying to get you behind the wheel of a car. You're scared. Well, that's good. The road is a dangerous place. But you've got wide-open tarmac as far as the eye can see here.' He gestured at the abandoned airfield. 'No one to hit. No one to run into you. Learn to handle the car at least.'

'You don't care whether I can drive, Jake. This is just another attempt to get me off your back.' Well, that got his attention. Took the 'casual' out of his laid-back posture. 'Listen to me. Hear what I'm saying. I'm not on your back. Go away and leave me in peace.'

'You want peace, but you don't give a hoot about my feelings, is that it?'

The space between her brows pulled together in a frown. 'What's that supposed to mean?'

'Think about it. See it from my point of view. You keep telling me to go, saying that you can handle it. Well, I want you to show me. Get in the driving seat and show me how capable you are. Because if you won't, Amy, I'm left with the conclusion that you're playing games with me. That this is all a sham. That no matter how much you keep saying go, you're determined to entangle me, keep me on side.'

'That's not true.' He shrugged, his gaze locked into hers, continuing to challenge her. 'I just can't—' Her voice broke.

'Why, Amy?' His voice was kitten-soft, his arms were strong about her and he pulled her close, cradled her against his chest.

'Please, Jake. Let it go.'

'Tell me why I should.'

It must seem such a small thing to him; he loved cars, motorbikes, handled them with consummate ease.

'My mother and sister were killed in a car accident,' she said, into his chest. He said nothing. Not reason enough? She looked up. 'I should have been dead, too.'

'I see. This is all to do with survivor guilt. The ''Why

me?'' thing.' She pulled away, shivered, and he opened the car door. 'Come on. Inside with you.'

She did as she was told, sat there numbly, with her arms tightly wound about her, while he walked around the car, climbed in beside her. 'Take me home,' she said.

He made no move to start the car. 'Your mother was driving?' he asked, matter-of-factly, as if he knew that gentleness would be a mistake. She continued to stare out of the window, but she knew he was looking at her. Waiting. Insisting on the whole story. So be it. She'd tell him and then he'd understand.

'She hated driving, especially at night, but my father was away,' she said, as quickly as she could, desperate to get it over with. Then he'd see why getting behind the wheel of a car was so utterly impossible. 'He was working in Scotland and Beatrice—'

'Beatrice? Your sister?'

'She was two years older than me and she was in the Christmas play at school. I didn't want to go. I was so jealous of her angel wings and the glittery stuff on her white dress and the make up. I was in the back being a miserable little brat.'

'How old were you?'

She swallowed, remembering it all. 'Um…six. Nearly six.' He reached out and his hand tightened over hers as if to steady her, reassure her. 'No one knows what happened,' she said, rushing on. 'We swerved. A dog, or a fox on the road, maybe, they said. They said in the newspaper that it was a miracle I wasn't hurt.' She frowned. 'My mother and my big sister were dead. Where was the miracle in that?'

'And your father?' He anticipated what was coming, could only guess at how hard it would be for her to say the words. But he needed her to tell him, needed her to open up, let him in so that he could share the hurt.

'He died in a car accident the same night—rushing home after being phoned at work and told that Mum…' Her voice caught. He waited while she took a breath. 'He was driving too fast. He shouldn't have been driving at all…' She turned and looked at him. 'But there was no one with him. No one to stop him. I think that he must have been crying. I expect that was it.' And her voice, that cool, even voice, finally faltered, cracked.

'It wasn't your fault, Amy,' he said, hating himself for making her remember, gathering her into his arms, holding her as hot, silent tears ran down his neck, soaked into his shirt. Her hair, scented with camomile, brushed against his cheek. Beneath his hands, her body shook as she struggled to hold back the pain. 'It wasn't your fault,' he said, again.

'Yes, it was.' She looked up and her eyes were clouded, grey, unhappy. He'd done that to her, selfishly making her remember so that he could forget. 'Don't you see? It was all my fault. I was sitting in the back of the car, whining and moaning because I wasn't old enough to be an angel in the school play. My mother was distracted. There was no fox. She turned to yell at me…'

'It wasn't your fault, Amy,' he said fiercely as he realised what she'd put herself through over years and years of regret, guilt. Never talking about it. 'You were a little kid and little kids whine. If you were being difficult, she should have stopped the car.'

'But—'

'Your mother didn't have to drive if she didn't want to. She could have asked a friend to take you all to the play. She could have called a taxi. It was her responsibility to get you there safely—'

'Don't blame her!'

'I'm not,' he said, holding her shoulders, facing her squarely. 'I'm not blaming her. I'm saying that you shouldn't blame yourself.'

'Easy to say.' She looked up, her lashes spiked with tears. 'I've tried to drive, Jake. I just can't do it.'

'Yes,' he said, firmly. 'You can.' He took out a handkerchief, wiped her eyes, blotted her cheeks. 'Being here is not what I wanted. I told you that. I tried to buy help for you so that I could keep my distance. Not get involved. But here I am, doing it myself because it's the only way you'll let me do anything for you. That's a heck of a big step for me. Won't you meet me halfway?'

Jake had forced from her a secret she'd kept guarded in her heart since the accident and he hadn't been shocked, or horrified.

And he was right; he'd come a long way for her. He was a thousand miles away from the man who'd stood on her doorstep and said he'd didn't do commitment. All this—reading the books, worrying about her wearing high heels, joining the Bunny Club—what was that if it wasn't commitment?

'Why?'

'Why do I want you to meet me halfway?'

'No, why is it such a big step for you? Why is it so difficult for you to become emotionally involved?'

He touched the corner of her mouth. 'Enough secrets for one day,' he said. 'Come on, I'll take you home. We'll get a take-out for dinner.'

'That's it? I'm let off the driving lesson?'

'For today.'

'And tomorrow?'

'That's up to you. Think about it. I won't pressure you, I promise.' He handed her his handkerchief. 'I'll make a bargain with you, though.' She waited. 'Learn to drive, and on the day you pass your driving test I'll tell you the story of my life. If you really want to know it.'

'Promise?'

He pressed his lips against her forehead and then he took her hand, and with her fingers he silently crossed his heart.

CHAPTER SIX

SIXTH MONTH. Baby is growing fast. She has eyelashes now, and her hearing is finely attuned so she'll be listening if you sing to her, or tell her a story.

THE yellow monster was parked outside and Jake was in the nursery when Amy climbed down from the bus at the end of a long day.

Her legs no longer able to keep up with her racing heart, she took the stairs at the sedate pace befitting her rapidly increasing girth. The door was shut to keep the smell of paint from filtering through the cottage. To keep her from seeing the nursery until it was completed and she could get the total effect. He'd made her swear, on her honour, not to peek.

She had smiled at that and, having explained what she'd had in mind, left him to it, indulging the kid in him.

She smiled now, despite her impatience. He'd done everything himself. It had taken weeks, working odd evenings, weekends when he could, turning up unexpectedly and making her heart turn over. And she'd been good. Kept her word. She hadn't even looked in the boxes of furniture that had arrived the week before and been stowed in the garage. Well, he'd locked the garage and taken the key.

She could hear him moving about, and about to call out, let him know that she was home, instead she leaned her cheek against the warm wood, indulging herself, letting her imagination drool over her own particular fantasy of Jake wearing nothing but a pair of ancient denim cut-offs and honest sweat.

Then she sighed. Fantasy was right. Impending fatherhood had effectively switched off the 'lust' buttons in Jake's head. The nearest he'd come to kissing her had been a brief touch to her cheek that put her in the same bracket as an elderly maiden aunt.

Not that it had made her feel like any kind of aunt. Jake, that close, had made her feel hot, and female, and inclined to rip her clothes off. So far, she'd restrained herself.

She smoothed her baggy sweater tight against her rapidly increasing bump and pulled a face. It was just as well: six months pregnant and looking it, she wasn't likely to have the same effect on Jake. About to knock and tell him that she was home, she changed her mind.

She'd wait until she'd showered, put on some fresh mascara and a new loose silk shirt that hung to her thighs in soft shape-blurring folds. Not until she'd got the cool, friendly mask firmly in place would she see him. A girl had her pride.

Better make that a cold shower.

Jake surveyed the nursery. It wasn't exactly what Amy had planned. Correction, it wasn't anything like she'd planned, which was why he'd made her promise not to look until it was finished. He knew she'd kept her word because…well…if she'd looked she wouldn't have been able to stop herself from demanding to know what the heck he thought he was up to.

She'd probably hate it.

She'd probably insist he did it all again.

Which wasn't all bad. It would mean he'd have to

keep coming back until he got it right. He didn't want to think about what that meant. He was afraid a psychologist would have a field-day with it, though.

He turned as he heard the shower running in the bathroom. Amy was home. For a moment he allowed his mind to wander. He knew the theory, knew how her body had changed, how she'd look with his baby growing inside her. But the mystery of it, the beauty of it haunted him as he thought about the water flowing over her skin and imagined how it would feel beneath his hands, his mouth. Imagined how she would look when he touched her...

He snapped back, rubbed his hands hard over his face as if to erase the pictures his mind tormented him with. He'd been spending too much time here. Rushing down most evenings, spending weekends with Amy when he should have been at his desk.

The heartless empty echo of his penthouse offered no temptation to return to London, but the nursery was finished, the new furniture installed. Even the old narrow bed where he'd lain awake on the occasional nights he'd stayed over, thinking about Amy, on the other side of the landing, had been carted off to the tip.

That was what he'd come for. To do the things she wouldn't let him pay someone else to do for her. She'd been right about that. Trying to buy peace of mind was cheap. Peace of mind came with the sweat of hard work, the muscle ache of doing something that said, I care enough to do this for you myself.

But staying longer would be self-indulgent, would put out all the wrong signals.

Nothing had changed.

He hadn't changed. He had other priorities, other responsibilities that needed his urgent attention. Things he'd let slip.

He'd go and put the pasta dish he'd made for her supper in the oven, then take a shower and leave. No fuss.

He backed out of the room, taking one last look around, then closed the door behind him. As he turned he collided with Amy, catching her shoulders as she struggled for her balance, clutching at the towel she'd wrapped about her.

'Oops,' she said, as a small plastic bottle slipped from her fingers. And then, as she met his gaze, she blushed.

On the nights they'd spent in the same house he'd been careful to avoid intimacy, too conscious of an attraction that refused to die down no matter how much cold water he threw at it.

But the peachy blush betrayed her and the heat of it enveloped him, found an immediate answering response from a body kept too long on a short leash.

'I seem to be a bit wobbly on my pins,' she said after a long moment in which neither of them moved.

'It's normal,' he replied on automatic. The thinking, reasoning part of him had been seized by the sudden thickening of sexual tension. The softness of her skin beneath his palms, soft moist lips that invited him to taste the sweetness within... 'Your hormones are softening and stretching your muscles and joints.' He knew it all off by heart now, could apparently spill it out without the need for rational thought. It was just as well. His mouth might be making sense, but his mind was taking a holiday... 'To make giving birth easier.'

'Oh,' she said, holding his gaze, keeping him fixed, enchanted. It was like the first time they'd met, and he felt the same charge, the same free fall desire, the same longing to take everything that her eyes promised. 'Is that all?' she asked, after a long moment when the silence rushed back, suffocating rational thought.

'All?' He didn't want her to move. 'No, it's not all,' he said, desperate to prolong the contact, keep her close. 'Your centre of gravity has shifted, too. Your balance is off beam...' Her hair was wet, clinging to her face, and as he watched a drip slid down a strand and after a seemingly endless pause finally dropped and ran down into the hollow beneath her shoulder, where it pooled for a moment, and as if in a trance he bent to scoop it up on his tongue. And was confronted with the soft folds of the towel tucked between her breasts. He stared at it for a moment. 'Take it off.'

Her eyes flickered uncertainly. 'What?'

'Take it off. The towel. I want to see you.' He looked up and her throat moved as she swallowed. 'Please...' Then his own throat tightened, closed down, shutting off the power of speech as she reached for the tail of the towel tucked between her breasts, her eyes never leaving his face as she pulled it loose, held it for a moment, then let it fall.

'Oh...' The sound exhaled from deep inside him and then for a long time he forgot to breathe. Her face had become lovelier as she'd taken on the bloom of approaching motherhood, but no amount of theory could have prepared him for the changes in her, warned him that she would have become so much more beautiful, enriched by nature's perfect curves.

His hands slid from her shoulders, over breasts that were fuller, riper, and he cradled them in his palms. They were smooth and white with a faint tracery of blue veins. He acknowledged them, saluted them with the tip of his tongue, and there was a sharp intake of breath as his mouth pulled on the nipples that would soon suckle his son.

His breath, or hers? He couldn't say, but sank to his knees, his hands sliding over the place where his baby was growing.

'Jake…' As he pressed his cheek against her abdomen Amy struggled to get the word past her throat. This was too much; she wanted him too much. She'd thought she was in control of this, but she wasn't. Another moment and she'd lose all sense and beg him…beg him… 'Jake…please…' She grasped his head between her hands.

Please, don't? Or, Please, don't ever stop? She didn't know what she might have said if Jake hadn't moved right then, if he'd looked up, seen the need burning from her eyes. Instead he eased back, reached for the towel and passed it to her, giving her a moment to wrap it about her as he retrieved the bottle of oil, fixing his gaze on the label. As if looking at her was somehow beyond him.

'Massage oil?' He straightened. His eyes flickered back to the label. 'Mandarin oil,' he said. 'This is to help with stretch marks, isn't it? I read about that…'

'You read too much,' she said, holding out her hand for the bottle.

He looked at her then, and his jaw muscles tightened as he surrendered the bottle. 'Maybe.' Then, 'Soft joints,' he reminded her. 'You need to be careful. Keep off those high heels you love so much.'

Careful? That was all he was bothered about? That she was being careful? She wanted to scream. No, worse, she wanted to weep. 'You're full of…theory, Jake. Morning sickness, green leafy vegetables, floppy muscles... Tell me, what other excitements have you got lined up for me?'

'Breathlessness, heartburn, leg cramps,' he said abruptly. 'Will that do to be going on with? Are you finished in the bathroom?'

'All done. I won't disturb you, Jake.'

Too late, he thought, as he stepped beneath the water. She'd already disturbed him. Fatally. He'd stayed too long, got too close. And just now...holding her, he'd come within a heartbeat of telling her that he loved her. Which couldn't be true. Love, he knew, was a word that had no meaning.

He flipped the water on to cold.

Hormones, nothing. Amy leaned back against her bedroom door and caught at her breath. It hadn't been pregnancy-driven hormones that had flipped the wobble button when she'd run into Jake on the landing. And when he'd touched her, kissed her breasts, laid his head against their growing baby, she'd come close to saying that if the offer was still open she would marry him whether he loved her or not.

Just to keep him close.

Even if she believed that he loved her—and she was sure he did—that would be a fatal mistake. He had to know it, too. Recognise it. Admit it. Say it out loud.

She hadn't thought it would be this hard. Take this long. If he could turn away after the way he'd touched her, if he could step back, detach himself—well, maybe she was wrong. She'd been so certain. That first time it had seemed as if their minds had touched. But now she just couldn't seem to reach across the space between them.

She wasn't simply succumbing to floppy muscles…her mental acuity was apparently fogged up with an excess of hormones, too.

She rubbed her palm across her wet cheek. She was losing him. She leaned back, eyes closed. No. It was worse than that. If he didn't understand what she felt for him, if he felt so little in return, she was going to have to ask him to leave.

Today she'd been good. She'd done nothing, said nothing, but a girl could only stand so much before she succumbed to temptation and started playing dirty.

This was a game that had to be played by the rules or no one would win.

'It's finished?' she asked.

'All done.' Jake opened the nursery door and stepped right back so that she wouldn't have to brush past him. The cold shower had been completely ineffective. One touch and he wouldn't be responsible…

'Jake…' Amy stared at the finished nursery. Then she closed her eyes, did a quick rerun of her mind's vision of sky-blue, soft rose-pink, the little touches of gold, the vision she had worked so hard to describe to Jake. Then she opened them again.

No. She hadn't imagined it. The room was a vivid, mind-blowing mix of red and black and white. And gold. He'd remembered the gold. The effect was stunning. The furniture, the walls, the linen. It wasn't the effect she'd planned, but…something made her look up at the ceiling.

'A black ceiling?' The words were startled out of her. She turned and looked at him.

'You hate it.'

He said the words lightly enough, as if it didn't matter. But she knew it did. He'd done this not to annoy her, or irritate her, but because of some vision of his own. Aware that he was watching her closely, gauging her reaction, she moved slowly about the room, touching everything.

The old single bed that she'd slept in as a child had gone. Instead there was a futon. A place for her to sit, or open out and lie alongside her baby. There was a cot, a changing station; new cupboards replaced the elderly wardrobe... She opened a cupboard and was unable to stop herself from reaching out to the rows of toys waiting for small hands to play with them.

She took a red-and-black spotted ladybird from a shelf—velvet and satin, beautifully tactile—and turned to him. 'It's different,' she said. 'Your designer dreamed this up?'

'No!' He stuffed his hands into his pockets, stared at the floor. 'I read an article in one of those baby magazines.' Baby magazines? He'd been reading baby magazines? 'Babies can't distinguish pastel colours. Did you know that? They're stimulated by—'

'Let me guess. Red and black and white.'

'If you hate it, I'll do it again the way you wanted it...' She brushed a tear from her cheek. 'Oh, God! You loathe it. Amy, I'm sorry! Don't cry, please don't cry. I'll change it. I'll do anything you like...'

She was shaking her head, looking up at him. 'You did this?' she asked. 'On your own?'

'Yes. I'm sorry. Please, sweetheart.' He wanted to put his arms around her, comfort her, but was afraid that it would just make things worse. 'I got carried away, excited. I wanted it to be...' She was standing in the middle of the room, just standing there, tears pouring down her cheeks. Nothing could make it worse. He reached out for her, held her. Damn! How could he have been so stupid, got so carried away with his own brilliant plans, not thinking, not caring about how she might feel? As if he didn't know. 'Amy, please don't cry. I'll fix it. I'll get someone in and you can have exactly what you want.'

'No.'

'No, you're right. I have to do it myself. I'll have to cancel my trip…'

'No, Jake. I don't hate it. It's just been a bit of a shock, that's all.'

'But you cried.'

'I cry all the time. I cried yesterday because a little girl let go of a balloon and it floated away.'

'Really?'

'Well, she cried first and it just set me off…' She sniffed. 'Vicki bought me a waterproof mascara.'

He lifted the hem of his T-shirt and wiped her eyes. 'That's what I call a friend.'

'Um.' She tightened her lips against her teeth and looked up. And tried not to shudder at the ceiling. 'What have you done with the light?'

'Oh! You haven't seen the best bit.'

'There's more?'

'The best bit.' He drew the heavy red curtains, darkening the room almost to night. 'You now have two light switches. Switch one,' he said. And downlighters illuminated the room, brilliantly. 'It's on a dimmer switch,' he said, and turned down the wattage until it was no more than a soft wash against the walls. 'And switch two.' The downlighters went off and the black ceiling was suddenly picked out with little points of light, like stars, that twinkled here and there.

For a long time she stood and watched. 'Did you really do all this, Jake?'

'The electrics?' He looked like a man torn between damning himself with truth or damning himself with a lie. 'I held the ladder,' he said, opting for the truth. 'You needn't worry...the guy was an expert.'

'I wasn't worrying... I'm just speechless.'

'Er... Is that good, or bad?'

'Come here.'

He crossed to her and she reached up, took his face between her hands and she kissed him. It was a sweet kiss, a kiss that said Thank you, and, I think you're amazing and for a moment it seemed as if it might be a whole lot more, but it was over so quickly that he might have got entirely the wrong idea...

'That means it's good, right?'

'I think it's incredible,' she said. Then, because he didn't look convinced, she added, 'It's amazing, imaginative, exciting. But the best bit—the very best bit—is that you've put yourself into the nursery. That's why I kissed you.'

Entirely the wrong idea... 'I did try the blue. For the sky. But that translucent colour you wanted just didn't work. Not the way you wanted it to. Sometimes it isn't possible to translate it from the imagination into the physical.'

Paint was one thing. She was something else. As far as Amy was concerned, the physical had outstripped his imagination by every measure known to man.

She was wearing a black poet's shirt, loose and baggy, that concealed all those wonderful curves, but his mind's eye was more than capable of filling in the details. His mind was giving him a seriously hard time.

'That's when I started looking around for something else. I knew it was radical—'

'It's certainly that.'

'Which is why I didn't want you to see it until it was finished. If you don't like it, Amy, I'll change it. Just promise me you won't be climbing any stepladders the moment my back's turned.'

Amy looked up. 'You said something about cancelling a trip. You're going away?'

Half an hour ago she had been sure that she should ask him to leave, but at the prospect her heart sank like a stone.

'I have to go to Brussels for a few days. A week, maybe. After that I'm heading for the Far East, coming back via California. I put it off for as long as I could—'

'Don't apologise, Jake. You've done everything you came for and more.' She'd miss him so much... But she mustn't cling. 'Mrs Cook will miss you,' she said.

That was it? 'Mrs Cook will miss me?'

'Cutting her grass.'

'Summer's nearly over,' he said brusquely. It was just as well. He couldn't stay. Wouldn't make the promises he didn't know how to keep. 'This isn't what I do, Amy.' He made a vague gesture in the direction of the nursery. 'I told you that.'

'I heard you. And you've been wonderful. I really appreciate you giving me so much of your time.'

Her voice was quiet. Barely there. Dammit, how dared she make him feel guilty? He'd warned her... 'You didn't leave me much choice.'

'That's not true, Jake.' She lifted her head a little, looked straight at him. And that was worse. 'The choice was always yours, but I'm happy you made the one you did. And I'm glad you made the nursery truly yours. I'll make sure Polly knows.'

'Polly?'

'It's a pet name for Mary. That was my mother's

name.' She stroked the bump. 'I'm going to call her Polly.'

'Funny name for a boy. I'd settled on George.'

There was a moment of silence before Amy said, 'I mustn't keep you. You must have a lot to do.'

Amy heard her quiet, measured voice saying all the right words while inside her head she was screaming. A week in Brussels! A whole week! Their baby would grow a centimetre, nearly half an inch, while he was there. And then he was going to the other side of the world…

After the last few weeks, his absence would be like a hollow pain. An empty space where there had once been his crooked smile, the unconscious touch of his hand on her arm any time he was close. She'd ache for those lightest of kisses on her cheek when he arrived out of the blue at the shop to take her out for lunch, or give her a lift home. She'd even miss the distracted way he pushed his fingers through his hair when he felt under pressure. He was doing it now…

Maybe he was right to go. If he was leaving it was better that he went sooner rather than later. She'd started to get used to him being around. Started to listen out for him, to rush home hoping he'd be there and, oh, the heart-lift when he was…

He'd fixed all kinds of things that had needed doing for ever. The garden looked wonderful. And she'd been good. She hadn't made even the feeblest of protests when he'd installed a clothes drier in the scullery without asking her first.

And he hadn't once raised the question of her learning to drive.

'How was your day?' he asked, obviously hoping to change the subject.

Her day had been difficult. Stressful. Oddly satisfying.

'I…um…took a driving lesson.' He turned to look at her, his face giving nothing away. She'd thought he would be pleased. Might even reward her with a kiss. Just a little one. On the cheek would do to be going on with. Anything could happen when they were that close. Anything almost had…

'A driving lesson?' he prompted.

Obviously not. Well, she was a big girl, she could handle it. She would have to. She was the one who didn't have any choice.

'Well, not a driving lesson exactly. I sat in the driving seat of a car and went through the controls.'

'That's a start.'

'I even managed to switch on the engine and move the car a few feet.' She smiled, ruefully. 'Unfortunately my leg was shaking so much that I stalled.'

'Well, that's to be expected.'

'Is it? The instructor said so, but I thought she was just being really, really kind. She was incredibly patient with me. We're having another go tomorrow.'

'Why?' he asked. 'Why are you putting yourself through this?'

She looked up at him. 'Because you'll feel better about leaving me. Because I wanted to convince you that you're truly free. That you don't have to stay for any reason.' Other than that he wanted to. She'd been fooling herself. He was already making plans to move on. 'To save you the embarrassment of having to drive that car yourself,' she said, forcing herself to make light of it. No point in saying the words if the face, the body language were saying something else.

'I was wrong, Amy. There's nothing sham about you.

Will you forgive me for accusing you of playing games with me, trying to entangle me, hold on—?'

'You were angry,' she said quickly, stopping him from saying the words. 'In your place I'd probably have felt the same. And I'm glad you said those things because it made me see things from your point of view. Made me think about what it would really be like on my own.'

Lonely.

She'd been on her own for years, ever since her grandmother had died. But she'd never felt lonely before. Without Jake...

She crossed to the window, pulled back the curtains and looked down on the small patch of lawn that would be just perfect for a swing. She'd only have to say the word and she knew it would appear. But Jake wouldn't be there to push it. Money couldn't buy you everything.

'I'll always be there, at the end of the phone,' he said, as if reading her mind.

'Will you? And if I phone and you're in California, or Japan, or Australia? Suppose the baby is sick, or later, when she's walking, she falls and hurts herself? What if I have to get to the hospital and there's no one around to help? I can't rely on someone just being available. Can I?' She turned and looked up as he joined her at the window. When he didn't answer she said, 'My imagination went into overdrive and I realised that you were right. I was being pathetic and selfish. Learning to drive was something I had to do.'

'I don't know what to say.'

She choked out a laugh. 'You're supposed to say, You could never be pathetic under any circumstances. Of course,' she rushed on, not giving him time to say anything, 'there's another, less noble motive.'

'Oh?' His brows knit together in a frown and she wanted to rub it away with the pad of her thumb. She restrained herself. Kissing him had been bad enough. Kissing him and wanting him to lose control and be the way he had when they'd made their baby—

'I'm determined to have your entire life story, chapter and verse. You haven't forgotten your promise?'

And, just in case he had, Amy took his hand and with his fingers drew a cross over her heart.

Jake could feel the heat of her skin through the silk and he opened his hand, pressed his palm against the slow, steady heartbeat that found a hot echo in his own pulse so that it was like a drumbeat in his ears.

Her mouth was soft, her lips slightly parted, her body ripe, his for the taking if he'd say the right word.

That word, he knew, was 'love'.

A word that had no meaning for him. Desire, he understood. Basic physical attraction that seized a man and held him briefly captive. But beyond that...

He wasn't going to pretend. Not to Amy.

As if she sensed something of what he was feeling, wanted to spare him more pain, Amy covered his hand with her own and, weaving her fingers through his, she carried it to her waist.

He didn't resist her, but as his hand curved over the swell of her abdomen the baby moved beneath his palm.

'Polly's been restless today,' she said.

'Behave, George,' he murmured. 'Give your mother a break while I'm away.' But his casual tone belied the jag of real pain, the bubbling up of long-suppressed anger as for the first time he fully comprehended the enormity of the emptiness within him.

'You're going now?' The words escaped before Amy could corral them. Needy little words that betrayed her.

'Pity,' she said, retrieving the situation with a careless shrug, and, turning away, headed for the stairs. 'I'd planned something special for dinner. To celebrate the start of my driving lessons. Smoked salmon...'

'Save the celebration until you've passed your test. I've made you some pasta. I was on my way to put it in the oven when—' He stopped. 'It'll only take twenty minutes.' He ducked under a beam as he followed her into her pretty living room, catching her hand and leading her to the sofa. 'I'll put it in and while it's cooking you can put your feet up and start learning your Highway Code.'

'No, leave it. I'll have it later,' she said, retrieving her hand, glancing at the clock. 'And I've already started learning the Highway Code.'

'You haven't got much time,' he said. 'Give Willow a ring; she'll help you with it.' He started for the front door. Then stopped. 'I've asked that old guy from the cottage down the road to come in and keep the garden tidy for you.'

'There's no need,' she said. 'Can you see my handbag? I put it down...' She spotted it on the hall table, picked it up.

'There's every need. He won't get paid until I get back, though, and I've made it quite clear that while he's welcome to work wherever he chooses, I'm only paying for what he does in *your* garden.' She gave him a reproachful look and he threw up his hands. 'All right, he can keep Mrs Cook's garden under control, since I won't be here to cut the grass, but that's it, Amy. He's saving up to visit his daughter in Canada, so he needs the money. Don't make it difficult for him.'

'That's so sneaky of you,' she said, taking her velvet cloak from the coatstand.

'I'm learning,' he said, trying not to concern himself with what she was doing. Where she was going.

He'd learned a lot. Not the gardening and DIY skills. He'd learned them long ago, when the excessive amounts of pocket money had abruptly stopped and the only way he'd been able to buy the things he wanted had been to work for them. Household chores, cutting grass, digging. Rough on a boy who'd never had to wash a dish, make his own bed, peel a potato in his entire life. This was different. This was doing something because you wanted to.

But he'd also learned that each day spent at the cottage chipped away at his resolve, his determination to do the right thing, put desire on hold and keep his distance.

That was why he was going away. To prove to himself that he was still capable of keeping his distance when every day seemed to make it tougher to remember why it was so necessary.

That was why he was leaving tonight, instead of to-morrow morning. Because one more night under the same roof as Amy Jones and he wouldn't be staying in the spare room. 'Are you going somewhere?' he asked, curiosity finally getting the better of him.

'Just into town.' She checked the time again. 'The bus goes in a couple of minutes. Give me a call when you get back; I'll tell you how much you owe Mr Thompson. No need to come yourself—'

'You're going into Maybridge?' he demanded, dropping his bag, blocking the door. 'What for?'

'Nothing.' He didn't move. She shrugged. 'If you must know, my antenatal classes start tonight.'

'And you weren't going to tell me?' He dismissed his own question as irrelevant. He'd just announced that he was leaving—and they both knew he wasn't planning on coming back—so why would she tell him? 'You can't go on your own.'

'Don't be silly, of course I can. I'll be perfectly safe—'

'I didn't mean that.' He didn't know exactly what he did mean. He stopped. Yes, he did. 'None of the other mothers will be alone.' They'd be arriving with their husbands, or their partners. Two people preparing together for a life-changing event. 'Will they?'

Amy's eyes widened slightly at his sudden sharpness. 'Probably…not. But these classes are to prepare for childbirth. You won't be there, so there's no point in you coming. Go and sort yourself out for your trip. I can manage,' she said, making light of it, dismissing his concerns with a smile. Her sweetness, her understanding would have softened an ogre's heart. And, despite his shortcomings, he was not an ogre.

'You shouldn't have to. You don't have to.' His head was telling him to stop. Now. He clearly wasn't listening because he heard himself say, 'I'll come with you tonight. Since I'm here.'

Amy felt guilty. Really guilty. She shouldn't have done it. She'd promised herself that she wouldn't. She could easily have waited until he'd gone and then called a taxi.

Telling Jake about the class was like saying those forbidden words: I need you.

That it was true had rocked her belief that she could do it all alone, the way she'd done everything important in her life. But this was different. She did need him with her; that was the honest truth. With every day that passed she needed him more. Not on the other side of the landing in the spare bed, but holding her, sharing this special time, sharing her life.

'Is that okay?' he whispered in her ear.

His arms were around her, his hands resting on their growing baby as they practised breathing techniques and she stopped worrying about Jake and instead snuggled back into his chest. This was probably about as good as it got. With their clothes on. She'd better make the most of it.

'Fine,' she said, covering his hands with her own. 'You?'

'It's different,' he conceded.

'You didn't have to come.'

'Am I complaining?'

'No. And I'm delighted you did. Thanks, Jake.' She turned her head to look back up at him. He wasn't exactly smiling. But his expression had an unwitting possessiveness that gave her a warm fuzzy feeling.

The feeling evaporated when after the class he drove her home, walked her to the door, but didn't cross the threshold. Not that he was in any great hurry to leave. He leaned against the porch, his hands stuffed in his pockets as if to keep them out of temptation as he stared up at the night sky.

'What'll you do for the next class?'

'I thought I might ask Willow to go with me. Be my birthing companion.' He kicked at a stone. 'Don't stress yourself out, Jake.'

He glanced at her. 'Easy for you to say.'

She sat down on the porch bench. 'Maybe. I don't know how to make it any easier for you.'

'Is that what you're doing? Making it easy?' He half smiled. 'Then heaven help me if you ever try to make it difficult.' Still he lingered. 'What's that scent?'

'Night-scented stocks. Nothing to look at, but they smell heavenly.' She forced herself not to offer him coffee. She might have made a vow not to break the rules, but she'd bent them way out of shape once tonight.

'Yes, well, I'd better be going.' He straightened, dragged his fingers through his hair.

'Take care, Jake.'

'I'll—' He'd been going to say he'd call her. Not a good idea. He was already too close. Tonight the class had gone through relaxation techniques and he'd listened to the stuff about breathing, massage, all the time holding her and knowing that he was different from those other men who were going to be there when their longed-for babies were launched into the world. He'd thought he'd put himself beyond all possibility of hurt. He was, apparently, wrong. 'I've left something for you. Well, something for the baby, I suppose. It's in the nursery.'

She said nothing. But as he walked quickly down the path, got into the car and drove away, he knew her green eyes would haunt him for ever.

The nursery was beginning to grow on her. Now she'd got over the shock. Jake's present was on the futon, a small parcel wrapped in gold tissue, and she picked it up, sat down and pulled on the red bow.

Inside was a poetry book, an anthology of favourite verses. And a CD of light classical music. Jake had enclosed a card.

According to all the books, babies have acute hearing and should be read to, and have music played to them. Jake.

Amy stared up at the ceiling, sighed. 'Idiot,' she murmured. But quietly, so that the baby wouldn't hear. For a moment, when she'd realised what he'd done with the nursery, she'd thought he'd broken through, made the leap of faith that was required for two people, almost strangers, to reach out and acknowledge a perfect affinity.

That was why she'd cried.

But then, when he'd so nearly been there, he'd taken a step back. She looked at the poetry book and sighed. Didn't he realise that his baby wanted to hear his voice reading the poems as well as hers?

She squeezed back the tears. She couldn't be angry with him because he was trying so hard. He was so caring. Imaginative. But he was so wrong.

She should have pressed him on his childhood. Whatever had happened to him must have been truly terrible to have robbed him of the ability to accept love when it was offered freely, unconditionally. To make him so resolutely determined never to become reliant on another person, never to surrender to his feelings. So determined never to have a child of his own.

Her imagination obliged with a dozen scenarios, each worse than the one before, and she cradled her swelling abdomen, as if to protect her restless unborn child from anything that terrible.

Her baby would have her daddy's present and know that she was loved. But Amy's throat was too tight, ached too much for her to read out loud. In her bedroom, she lit a scented candle, slipped the CD into her stereo and stretched out on her bed.

'Listen, angel, this is a present from your daddy,' she murmured, gently smoothing a blend of mandarin and camomile oil over her bump as the opening notes of

Brahms' 'Lullaby' whispered softly into the room. 'You see how much he loves you? He's thinking about you all the time, and while he's away he's going to miss you so much that when he comes home he'll want to read those poems to you himself.'

And because her baby could hear her, she put all the belief she could muster into her voice. She only wished she felt that confident.

CHAPTER SEVEN

SEVENTH MONTH. The growing baby will be creating pressure on your bladder and your stomach. You'll feel a little breathless, suffer from heartburn and maybe leg cramps. Your baby's eyes will now be open.

DISTANCE made no difference. Time did not help. Jake thought about Amy every waking moment. Constantly converting the time difference so that he would know where she was, what she was doing. He couldn't stop himself from wondering if she was persevering with the driving lessons. If she'd really liked the nursery. Or if the minute his back was turned she'd set about changing it.

Probably.

She was probably up that old stepladder with a pot of blue paint right now. His gut clenched at the thought. He should have burned it.

He should forget it.

He was walking through a shopping mall with a list faxed to him by Maggie. It seemed as if the kid of every employee had put in a request for some special item of sportswear or clothing for him to bring back from the States.

He could have sent someone out to do it for him, but it was the weekend. He had nothing better to do, and hunting down a football jersey was a distraction of sorts. He looked about him, scanning the shop fronts. And saw the cradle.

It was at the heart of a display of designer baby stuff. Not for sale, it had been put there to catch the attention of the casual shopper. As it had caught his. A genuine backwoods piece, hand hewn and well used, it took him straight back to that moment when Amy had stopped to look at another period piece when they'd walked together through the streets of Maybridge. They were a world apart, yet the feeling that had gone into them was the same.

And he knew why he hadn't offered to buy Amy the one in the antiques shop. There wasn't enough money in the world to buy what it represented.

Could he make one? He'd done basic woodwork at school. Once lodged in his brain, the idea took hold, firing him up. It would be something personal, something precious for Amy to keep and pass on to her grandchildren.

His grandchildren, he realised with a shock.

Mike. He'd call Mike. He'd know, help with a design... Back at the hotel, he reached for the phone, punched in the number. Willow answered.

'Jake! How wonderful. I thought you were in the States.'

'I am, darling. California. And I promise you it's neither cold nor damp—'

'Oh,' she said flatly. 'You're still there. I thought, I hoped, you'd come home when you heard about Amy—'

'What?' He felt his blood chill. 'What about Amy? What's happened?' Cold fingers feathered his spine. 'Is it the baby?'

'The baby's fine. Really. You're not to worry.' Her pause was judged to have entirely the opposite effect.

'Willow! Tell me!'

'She just had a bit of an accident, that's all—'

'*What kind of an accident?*' He was shouting, he realised. 'What kind of an accident?' he repeated, more gently.

'It's nothing. Honestly. Her knee…' The ladder; she'd fallen off the ladder. He'd told her, but would she listen? 'And her shoulder. But her head was okay. They took an X-ray as a precaution—'

'Willow, for the love of Mike, where have they taken her?'

'It was just a minor collision, Jake. No one else was hurt—'

'Collision?' The fingers stopped playing along his spine and he went cold all over. 'She didn't fall off the ladder?' The chill intensified. She'd been driving. She'd had an accident while learning to drive. Something she was only doing because he'd forced her into it. 'Where did they take her?' he repeated, grabbing his suitcase, one-handedly flinging in his clothes.

'Maybridge General, but…'

'But?' He stopped. 'There's something you're not telling me. She's lost the baby, hasn't she?'

'No…no… Everything's going to be fine…' There was another hesitation that did nothing to reassure him. 'I'm looking in whenever I can. We all are. You're not to worry, Jake, really—'

She kept saying that, but how could she imagine he wouldn't?

Perhaps because he'd been doing everything he could to distance himself from involvement with Amy since the moment he'd learned she was pregnant?

'I'll be home on the first available flight,' he said, cutting her short. 'In the meantime I want you to see that she has absolutely everything she needs.'

'Well, yes, of course…'

'Everything,' he insisted. 'I'll call my secretary at home and she'll be in touch with you about getting her moved into a private room—'

'But, Jake—'

'I'll be there in twenty-four hours.'

Willow replaced the receiver, turned to Mike, who'd just come in from the garden with Ben.

'That was Jake,' she said.

'Really? I thought he was still in America.'

'He is.'

'Oh. What did he want?'

'I've no idea. He must have forgotten when I told him about Amy's accident. He seemed very upset.'

He pulled a face. 'She said not to do that, Willow.'

'No, darling, what she said was that we weren't to ring him and tell him about the accident. I didn't. He rang me. He said we were to get Amy anything she needed.'

'And?'

She grinned. 'Sorted. He'll be here tomorrow.'

Jake regarded the hospital receptionist with disbelief. 'What do you mean, she's not here? She's had an accident. She's pregnant,' he added desperately, as if that might jog something loose in the woman's memory.

'That's right,' she replied with a practised calm that was presumably supposed to soothe distraught friends and relatives. It was having quite the opposite effect on him.

'So where is she?'

'According to my records she was treated in Casualty on the eighteenth.'

'And then?' he prompted, with what he considered commendable restraint, considering the provocation.

'And then she was sent home.'

'Home? But—' Didn't she understand? This was serious. He'd flown six thousand miles because…well, it was that serious. The woman, rushed off her feet, wasn't interested in his 'but'. She was already dealing with another query.

Home. He pushed open the back door of the cottage and it felt just like that. Coming home.

Except nothing was quite as it should be. The mud room was uncharacteristically tidy. Amy's gardening boots had been scraped clean and polished, for heaven's sake. He glanced around and saw that everywhere was immaculate. Cold. There was usually music, warm kitchen smells, activity of some kind, and the quiet emptiness was disquieting.

'Amy?' he called. The polished surfaces echoed back at him.

He ducked under the beam and Harry looked up from his cushion, sighed and then put his head back on his paws.

'Amy!' he called again, with more urgency. The back door had been open, so someone must be at home. Maybe she was upstairs, unable to move, unable to call out…

He took the stairs in three long strides. All the doors were shut, but he didn't stop to knock, bursting through her bedroom door. The rush of relief, of joy when he saw her, propped up on the bed, a heap of soft knitting on her lap, listening to music through her headphones, was so powerful that it momentarily took his breath

away. He couldn't speak. Remained frozen in the doorway.

'Jake!' She put the knitting aside, pulled off the headphones, leaving her hair sticking up in a little quiff. She
was bereft of make-up, wearing a long football jersey
that had seen better days and a pair of old jogging pants
that had been cut off above the knee on one leg. She
looked absolutely wonderful. Beautiful. The best thing
he'd seen in a long time—or, more accurately, since he'd
left her at the cottage door weeks—no, a lifetime—ago
and flown away.

'Don't move,' he said, finally regaining the use of his
vocal cords as she struggled to rise. 'I want to remember
you always, like this. With a packet of frozen peas
draped over your knee.'

She took the defrosting vegetables from her knee and,
ignoring his order not to move, threw them at him. He
caught them, dropped them, then crossed swiftly to the
bed, sitting beside her as she eased herself up, quickly
biting back a wince of pain. Not quickly enough.

'You're in pain. You should be in hospital.'

'It's nothing.' She made a dismissive gesture. 'I didn't
know you were back—'

'I came straight from the airport. And I told you not
to move.' He reached round her, fluffed the pillows. 'Lie
back.'

She subsided without protest, slipping down between
his arms, her head on the pillow, looking up at him with
eyes like molten emeralds, eyes that were hot, and dark,
and inviting. It was an invitation his body responded to
with an eagerness that left him gasping for breath.

He wanted to kiss her, really kiss her. None of that
polite, big brother kiss-on-the-cheek stuff he'd been con-
gratulating himself on doing so well. He wanted her lips

beneath his tongue, he wanted to taste her, look at her, hold her and their baby. And never let them go again.

'Can I get you anything?' he said abruptly, sitting back.

She swallowed, as if she too had felt the charge, the heat. 'A fresh ice pack would be good,' she said.

Her voice shook a little, and it was taking every ounce of his self-control not to simply take her into his arms and tell her how much he'd missed her, how he'd be there for her, always. He owed her a lot more than easy words. A lot more than he could ever offer her.

Better make that two ice packs. One for her, one for him.

'Any particular flavour?' he asked, keeping it light. 'Broad beans, perhaps? Or maybe diced carrots would make a change?'

There was a small still moment, then she said, 'The choice is peas or peas. Dorothy got them from the village shop and she doesn't believe in unnecessary complications.'

'She's in the wrong place, then.' He retrieved the soggy packet from the floor. 'She's looking after you?'

'Like a mother hen,' she said, with a look that suggested she didn't find being a 'chick' an entirely pleasing experience. 'If you'd just put those back to refreeze and bring another one, I'd be eternally grateful.'

'That would be a first.' He was the one who should be grateful, he thought as he went down to the kitchen. Grateful for the chance to escape, get his libido back under control, get his head straight. He couldn't quite make it. 'Where is Dorothy?' he asked when he returned, as he placed the fresh pack carefully over her swollen knee, taking the opportunity to check out the damage and trying not to notice that her beautiful ankles hadn't swollen a bit.

'It's the pensioners' lunch club today. She's helping out.'

'She should be here, with you.'

'That's what she said, but I really needed a break. Dorothy is a wonderful woman, but she has this thing about polishing. Everything squeaks it's so clean. Poor Harry has been banned from the bedroom altogether.'

'Is that why he's looking so fed up? Shall I fetch him?'

'Later,' she said. She moved the bundle of knitting, dumping it in a basket beside the bed, and then patted the bed. Not the edge, where he'd sat so briefly, but the wide inviting space at her side. 'I really need some human company. Come and put your feet up, tell me what you've been doing.'

'Nothing,' he said, staring at the double bed with longing. 'Working, mostly.' If only the longing was simply for rest. But he'd been on the move for twenty-four hours and was bone weary, so despite that swift jag of desire it would probably be all right. He peeled off his jacket, kicked off his shoes and lowered himself carefully beside her so as not to disturb her knee.

'Successful trip?' she asked.

'I'm not here to discuss business,' he said, stretching out on his side, propping himself on his elbow so that he could look at her. He needed to feast on the sight of her, reassure himself that she was safe. He reached out for her hand and she met him halfway, carried his hand to place it on their growing baby, covering it with her own. The closeness came as a shock after weeks of abstinence, of keeping his distance, and he closed his eyes as he remembered his mouth on her breasts, his face

against the swell of their growing child. Then tried to
shut it out. Too late. 'I want to know what's been happening to you,' he said thickly.

'Me? I'm just a total fraud. If it wasn't for this stupid
knee—'

'And the "stupid" bang on the head,' he said, bending to touch the bruise darkening her forehead with his
lips. 'Not forgetting the "stupid" bruised shoulder.' He
resisted the urge to kiss that better, too. Who knew
where that kind of thing might lead to?

'Uh-oh... Someone's been telling tales,' she said,
brushing off her injuries with a laugh, making a joke of
it.

'It's not funny, Amy. I went racing to the hospital
expecting to find you at death's door—'

'Did you?' She frowned. Then groaned. 'Oh, no.
Please don't say you came rushing home just because
someone told you I'd had an accident? I mean, as accidents go, it was a pretty minor affair.'

'Willow may have omitted to tell me that you'd been
treated as an outpatient,' he agreed. 'But when you're
pregnant no accident can be considered minor.'

'Willow?' She lifted her free hand in a helpless little
gesture, pushing back a thick cowlick of pale gold hair.
'Not Dorothy?'

'No, and I'll be asking her why she didn't think it
necessary to call my office when I see her. I rang Maggie
every day—' He stopped. He'd rung Maggie every day
to check for messages. Just in case. He should have been
phoning Amy.

When he didn't continue, Amy said, 'You musn't
blame Dorothy, Jake. She was going to ring your office—'

'So why didn't she?'

She lowered her lashes. 'Poor Dorothy. I'm ashamed to tell you.'

'But you will.'

'Will I?' She glanced sideways at him, from beneath a fringe of lashes that should have had a health warning attached. As should her eyes. She could switch from go-to-hell wicked to little-girl innocent in a second. Right now they were all innocence, but he wasn't fooled for a moment. He responded to her challenge with nothing more than a lift of his brows. 'I was really bad, Jake.'

'So what's new?'

She pulled a face. 'I refused to eat the chicken soup, or the lightly boiled egg, or any of the other good things she assured me were absolutely essential for my recovery until I extracted her solemn promise not to call you. You know Dorothy. She's not the kind of woman to break a promise.'

'That was bad,' he agreed. 'Pity about Willow.'

'Yes. I assumed she had more sense than to bother you with something this minor.'

'She didn't call me. I rang her,' he said. 'Or rather I rang Mike. About something else entirely. It's just as well, since there seems to have been a conspiracy to keep me in the dark.'

'Nonsense.' She shrugged. 'Dorothy put up a spirited fight, but in the end even she had to agree that whilst this—' she pointed at her knee '—might be incapacitating and painful and a monumental nuisance, it's nothing to make a transatlantic drama about.'

'I'll be the judge of that.' He shifted the pillows at his shoulders, settling down to make himself more comfortable. Getting closer. 'Tell me about it.'

'There's nothing to tell.' He didn't respond to this obvious understatement, simply lifted his hand in a gesture that said, Please be serious. 'Well, not much. It was all so stupid. The bus was pulling into a stop and I—'

'You drove into a bus?'

'What?' She looked down at him, frowned. 'No, of course I didn't. I didn't drive into anything. I'm an excellent driver. I've already passed my written test. That entitles me to half your life story, by the way—'

'No, it doesn't, sweetheart. All or nothing.'

'Oh, be fair! I've had to cancel my test!'

He wasn't falling for that. 'Don't change the subject. The bus was pulling into a stop. If you didn't hit it, what did you do?'

'Nothing! I was a passenger. I was on my way to the antenatal clinic. Just a routine check-up,' she added, before he could ask.

'And you haven't heard of taxis, I suppose?'

'If we don't support our local bus service, Jake, we'll lose it.' She waited for an argument, but he didn't waste his breath. 'Anyway, the bus was pulling into my stop. I'd just got up when a child dancing around at the bus stop toppled off the kerb. The driver hit the brakes and I lost my balance. She wasn't hurt,' she reassured him. He said nothing, but she was apparently reading his mind, because she said, 'I'd have been all right, too, but for the wobbly muscles and the dodgy centre of gravity.' She paused, waiting for him to smile. He didn't. 'It's nothing, Jake.'

But it could have been everything. On the long flight from California he'd managed to scare himself witless thinking about just how bad it could be. How empty the world would be without Amy somewhere in it. Without their baby.

'It isn't nothing. You were hurt.'

'Yes, well, it's just a twisted knee—and when I say

just a twisted knee I want you to know that I'm being forbearing and patient and incredibly noble here—'

'What about the baby? No after-effects? You've seen a specialist?'

'She's fine.'

'You're sure?'

'You don't have to take my word for it.' She reached across and took a small folder from the night table and handed it to him. 'See for yourself.'

He opened it up and was confronted with an image that for a moment didn't mean anything to him. Then it did, and the earth turned while he forgot to breathe.

'Is this what I think it is?'

'It's a picture of your daughter at thirty-two weeks old. They did a scan, just to be on the safe side.'

His daughter. Until now the idea of the baby had been a vague, remote idea. Something to be dealt with on a practical level. But to see the reality of her, a tiny hand, fingers. He swallowed, reached out blindly, and Amy caught his hand.

'It's incredible…'

'I know. She's amazing, isn't she? I've been playing her the CD you bought her, and I've been reading to her from the poetry book.' She took his hand and placed it on the place where her baby lay beneath her breast. 'She's awake. Listening to your voice. Talk to her, Jake.'

He opened his mouth, but couldn't think of a thing to say. He didn't know how to speak to his child. He'd had no example to follow. No childhood legacy of soft words to draw on, no deep memory well of paternal affection to draw on.

'I'm amazed at how much bigger you are,' he said.

Her sigh was little more than a breath. Then, holding his hand against the curve of her belly, as if willing him to embrace the baby she was carrying, she quipped, 'Nothing to choose between me and a hippopotamus.'

'A very small hippopotamus,' he replied.

'How kind.'

No. Guilt wasn't kindness. But he couldn't expect her to understand. No one could understand. It wasn't that he didn't care, didn't know how important this small life was.

He knew only too well. But he also knew how easy it was to inflict hurt—not physical hurt, but the careless kind that left no visible scars, no bruises. Just, nothing. A legacy he had determined never to pass on.

'I can't believe how time has flown,' he said, abruptly changing the subject. 'You're still set on a home delivery?'

'It's all arranged. The midwife is booked, Sally is standing by—' Beneath his hand the baby shifted, the movement unexpectedly powerful, and he looked up in surprise. Amy was watching him. 'She turned over,' she explained. 'She'll sleep now.'

'Babies sleep?'

'Of course.'

'And they said it was definitely a girl?' He looked at the scan again. He was no expert but he'd have said otherwise.

'I didn't ask. I know it's a girl. Do you mind?'

About to say that it made no difference to him, he thought better of it. He was no longer sure what he felt beyond a desperate longing that the child should be strong and happy. And, of the two, he thought happy was the most important. But she was waiting for an answer.

'So long as it's one or the other.'

'I think I can manage that,' she said, but he thought

that she smiled out of politeness, and perhaps to hide her disappointment that he couldn't have shown a little more passionate involvement.

He longed to tell her that it was the most important thing in the world to him. He was no longer sure what he felt. The rollercoaster of fear, exhaustion, relief, was just too much. He needed a shower. He needed to put some space between them before he said something that he could never recall and knew he would immediately regret.

'A girl is fine. But I think you're fooling yourself,' he said, returning the picture to her. 'That is without doubt a boy.'

'If it's a boy, you can choose his name.'

'George it is then.'

She smiled indulgently. 'You look as if you're about to drop, Jake. Take a nap if you want to. Dorothy's taken the futon into my office. She found the nursery decor a little too stimulating,' she explained, 'so I'm afraid you'll have to bunk up with me.' Then she grinned. 'But, hampered as I am by my injuries and imminent maternity, you'll be quite safe.' Thus neatly implying she didn't expect him to be in the least bit turned on by her.

She was underestimating herself.

He might be safe from her physical presence, but inside his head he didn't feel safe. Just to think of her was taking a risk. 'You could use more room,' he said, not so much changing the subject as shifting it sideways. 'You'll need somewhere for a nanny.'

'I don't need a nanny.'

'Be realistic, Amy.' On her own with a baby, running a growing business, she'd have to have live-in help. 'You could use your office for the time being, I suppose…'

'It's not big enough for a baby, let alone a nanny. And I need my home office even more now.'

'Oh?'

'This accident has forced me to rethink my plans. I've put Vicki in charge of the shop full-time; I'm going to concentrate on the postal and internet business.'

'Well, that's something, I suppose. And Vicki's right about the name. Why don't you franchise it?'

She glanced at him thoughtfully. 'Put an ''Amaryllis Jones'' in every high street?'

'Why not? The black and gold image is very powerful and the name is memorable.'

'Even jet-lagged you're a money machine, aren't you?' She didn't sound particularly pleased. 'Do you ever stop thinking about business?'

'Everyone should be good at something, and since you won't take my money I'll have to concentrate on making you a millionaire in your own right. Leave it with me. I'll make some enquiries. But you are still going to need more room here.'

'I'll convert the attic one day, when Polly needs a study, somewhere to be private.' She smiled. 'There's no rush.' And, having evoked an image of his daughter as a teenager, with a life of her own, secrets, boys falling in love with her, she lay back against the pillows and stroked the curve of her belly.

'There's always less time than you think, Amy.' Then, because he wasn't letting her off scot-free, 'And George will need somewhere to lay out his train set.'

'What train set?'

'The one I'm going to buy him the day he's born. Isn't that what fathers are supposed to do?'

'Right after passing round the cigars,' she agreed, with undisguised amusement. 'Thanks for racing home, Jake.

I really needed a laugh. I'm sure Polly will love having a train set to play with.' She kissed his brow. 'And I appreciate your concern.'

Concern? Did she really think he'd felt something as pallid and milksop-weak as simple concern? The feelings that had raged through him had been far more complex, extraordinarily powerful. New.

Tenderness, fear, a fierce protectiveness.

'Yes, well, maybe I overreacted a little,' he said, mentally stepping back from the brink, rubbing his hand over his face. He was tired, and she was right; he'd been concerned. His imagination had been working overtime, that was all. 'Willow was uncharacteristically vague.'

'How unlike her. Was it a bad line?'

It had been as clear as a bell between Upper Haughton and Silicon Valley... Maybe between his ear and his brain the message had got a bit scrambled. Maybe guilt had clouded his usual clarity of thought. Willow's lack of lucidity might have been intentional, but he hadn't asked any of the right questions. Maybe he hadn't wanted reassurance. Maybe he'd just wanted an excuse to come home. He closed his eyes. *Home.*

'Jake?'

'Mmm?'

Her fingers feathered his forehead, his temples, his cheeks, and his last coherent thought was that he was being stroked with rose petals.

Amy saw Jake's heavy lids succumb to gravity with considerable relief. He looked terrible, as if he'd been pushing himself beyond endurance for too long. Or maybe flying nonstop from California accounted for his hollowed eyes, the drawn look about his mouth.

Crazy.

He could have phoned Dorothy. Called his secretary. Jumping on the first aircraft was...promising.

She murmured his name. 'Jake?' He mumbled something unintelligible from the slow slide into sleep and turned onto his back.

She smiled, reached for the scented oil on her night table. The blissful scent of rose absolute was reputed to ease emotional stress, and she'd been giving it a pretty tough workout since Jake had driven off into the night weeks ago.

She poured a little into her palm, spread it over her hands and then stroked her lightly oiled fingers over his forehead, smoothing out the lines, brushing her thumbtips over his temples. Her fingertips grated over his unshaven chin, the hollow cheeks. He'd lost so much weight that she'd been hard pushed to hide her shock when she first saw him.

She stroked his neck, eased her fingers beneath his collar and over his shoulders, and gradually she felt the tension slip away from him as he sank into a dreamless sleep. Then she carefully unbuckled his belt and slipped it through the loops, before unfastening the button at his waist and lowering herself down beside him. Her shoulder was touching his, her foot was resting against his ankle and, since he was asleep and wouldn't ever know, she slipped her fingers through his.

The door was open and after a while Harry leapt onto the bed, purring loudly, pounding at the cover with his paws until Jake stirred, turned over, and settled with his face pressed up against her breast.

Amy put her arm around him, gently kissed his forehead and watched him sleep.

CHAPTER EIGHT

EIGHTH MONTH. The good news is that your baby is growing steadily. The bad news is that the heartburn is getting worse, your ankles may be swollen and you feel slightly less graceful than a hippopotamus. Keep emergency numbers close at hand.

JAKE stirred, drifting slowly up from the depths of sleep with a feeling of well being. An unaccustomed peace. And when he opened his eyes he knew why. He was in Amy's bed. He was home.

It got better. He was naked in Amy's bed. Sadly he had no recollection of getting that way. He looked at his wristwatch and groaned. It was nearly two o'clock and the thin, watery sun creeping over the windowsill made that two in the afternoon.

He needed a shower, he needed to call his office—be in his office—but mostly he needed to see Amy. As his own bag was still downstairs, he unhooked a roomy bathrobe from behind the door, wrapped it about him and went in search of her.

She was in her tiny office at the far end of the landing, her leg propped up on a cushioned chair as she worked at her computer. She turned, smiled at him, and he forgot why it had ever seemed so important to leave.

For a smile like that, he'd have swum the Atlantic.

'Hi,' he said.

'Hi.'

'I think I slept the clock round.' It wasn't quite a question, but she answered it for him anyway.

'Very nearly. You woke just before midnight, drank a pint of water and got into bed. When I say woke, your eyes were open but I don't think anyone was at home.'

'I don't remember,' he admitted.

'You were tired.'

'If I was in bed with you naked and I don't remember, sweetheart, I was comatose. Were you naked, too?'

'That's for me to know and you to wonder about,' she said, never missing a beat, but her cheeks warmed a little; his blood heated in response as his imagination filled in the gaps. 'You look better for the rest,' she said, firmly changing the subject.

He ran a hand over his jaw. 'I look terrible. I need a shower and a shave. Maybe then we could try it again to, you know, jog my memory?'

The delicate flush deepened and she turned quickly away. 'You can't remember where the bathroom is?'

Then she stilled, glanced quickly back, and for a moment they were both remembering. Not the passion, the need, the total recognition of two people in tune for one perfect moment in time. But afterwards. The way he'd stormed up to the bathroom looking for confirmation of overheard gossip, confirmation that she was pregnant. They were remembering his anger. What he'd said.

He remembered with shame, barely recognising the man he'd been.

'First door on the left,' she prompted, after a long pause, when he still didn't move. Then, 'Are you staying, Jake? I'll have to let Dorothy know about dinner...'

'Do you need me to stay?'

Amy felt the excitement, the pleasure, the joy of his return trickle away. He was asking, which was an improvement, but nothing else had changed; he still wanted to go.

'No, Jake,' she said. 'As you see, the mercy dash was quite unnecessary.' She smiled and thought her face would crack with the effort. 'Welcome, but...'

'Unnecessary. If you're sure? It's just that I didn't tell anyone what I was doing. It was the weekend—' He glanced at his watch. 'I should put in an appearance at the office before the rumours start flying. You know how it is. The boss goes missing for twenty-four hours and everyone thinks the company's going down the pan and panics.'

'I understand. You have responsibilities.'

'It's my company, Amy.'

'You like to be in control.' It wasn't a question. She didn't expect an answer. The one she got surprised her.

'So do you,' he said.

'No...' Then, 'Well, maybe.' She extended a hand to him and when he took it she squeezed lightly before pushing him away. 'If you want something to eat before you leave,' she said, turning back to her computer, 'Dorothy will see to it.'

'Amy.' She continued to stare at the screen but he could see her reflection, the tightening jaw, the swift blink that betrayed her battle against tears. 'It's me, not you. I'm the problem. You're everything a man could hope for, desire...'

'If a man was capable of commitment.'

'You don't understand...'

'No?' She turned then and he saw that she'd lost the battle, that her cheeks were damp. But her mouth was soft. 'Maybe I would. If you told me.' She waited, and when he didn't move, turn away, she pressed on. 'Whatever happened to you, however much you were hurt, you don't have to let it rule your life. You can change, take control—'

'I am in control.'

'No, darling, you just think you are. You're walking a line someone else drew. You can step off it any time you want.'

'It's too late. I am what fate made me.'

'You can be whoever you want to be. You choose. You can be a man who by some accident of fate creates a child, an inconvenience to be brushed aside, forgotten as easily as your parents forgot you.'

He felt his blood run cold. 'I'll never forget—'

'Or you can be a father.'

'What does that mean?'

'You know what it means,' she said. 'Deep down where it matters. A father is someone to hold a tiny hand when a child takes her first steps. A father is always there, someone to cling to when she's scared, someone to cheer her on at school sports day and cuddle her when she comes in last. He frets when she's out on her first date with a boy he just knows is going to break her heart, because he was once that same boy. And he's there, with an arm to support her, to lead her down the aisle on the biggest day of her life.'

'I don't know how to do that! How do you learn that when no one has ever been there for you?'

'You just reach out, Jake…there'll be someone there to take your hand and show you the way.'

And if he did? There would be no going back. No putting back together the carefully constructed façade that he'd built to protect himself. It would be like stepping into the dark. Never had the prospect appeared more enticing. Or terrifying.

Amy watched his internal struggle. She could see the

battle warring behind eyes darkened with remembered pain. Hampered by her leg, she was unable to go to him, touch him, hold him, comfort him. She should have stayed in bed with him, been there when he woke to hold him, show him that love wasn't something to fear, that it didn't steal your soul, but filled it with sweetness...

She'd told herself that it wouldn't be fair. Wouldn't be playing by the rules. Maybe, though, she'd been afraid, too. Just a little bit terrified that she'd been fooling herself and that he wouldn't want to wake up and find her at his side.

That was new. The uncertainty, the fear that she'd got it all wrong. Beside her, the phone began to ring. She ignored it for as long as she could, trying to keep Jake focused on what she'd said. Not for her, but for him. But the drilling sound was too much and she snatched it up. 'Yes?'

'Miss Jones? Maggie Simons, Jake's secretary. We appear to have, er, lost him. I wondered if you could help?'

'Yes. He's here.' She tossed the phone to him. 'Saved by the bell. It's your secretary. The outside world is looking for you.'

'Maggie... I'm sorry... Yes, I know I should have left a message... All right! I'll be there.' He hung up. Looked at her. 'I have to go.'

'Sure you do. You'll find the number for the local taxi firm on the fast dial.' Amy's voice was brisk, bright; she was apparently more interested in what was on the screen in front of her as she mentally pushed him away.

The first time she'd done that he'd been confused. Now he knew exactly what she was doing and he finally

understood how much it was costing her. And for once
in his life he wasn't thinking in financial terms.

'I'll be back, Amy.' Her fingers were flying over the
keyboard and she didn't turn round. 'I'll be busy for a
day or two, but if you need anything, anything at all,
just call me. And stay off buses,' he added, just a touch
desperately. Anything to regain her attention. 'Take a
taxi to the clinic. Anywhere. I'll open an account.'

That did it. 'Anything. Anywhere.' She swung round
to face him. 'How easy life must be when you can just
open an account and write a cheque at the end of the
month to clear away all your problems.'

He'd got her attention and more. She'd finally let the
mask slip and shown him a glimpse of the pain he'd
caused her, let him see far more than she'd ever intended. The flash of heat from her eyes was like the heat
from an oven door opened quickly to check on a cake,
then closed. A blast of warmth, the promise of something wonderful.

'I can't promise...' He heard the mean little words,
words he'd heard all through his childhood and which
were somehow ingrained on his soul. 'But I'll try to get
down at the weekend.'

Try? Amy heard the word and knew that it was over,
because if their situations were reversed she'd have to
be tied to her desk to keep her from flying to him the
moment she could. Nothing would keep her away. But
a promise would mean commitment.

And finally she heard what he'd been saying since the
moment they'd met. Acknowledged that he'd already
gone way beyond anything that he'd ever bargained for.
That this was as good as it was going to get.

'Why, Jake?'

For a moment the gentleness of her voice fooled him.

Then he realised that this was no casual question. There was no smile, just a silence stretching on and on like a rubber band being pulled to breaking point.

'Why?'

Repeating the question had been a bad idea, as like a rubber band it flipped back and stung him.

'If it's so hard for you, why would you bother coming back at all?'

She was absolutely still, waiting, insisting he answer. Inside Jake's head, the cogs were whirring, disengaged. He knew what he had to say but it was as if the words were some foreign language.

When the silence became so thick that it was a presence in the tiny room, she made the smallest movement, scarcely more than a lift of her fingers. 'I'm sorry, Jake, I'm going to be busy this weekend.'

'Amy—'

But she had already turned back to her computer.

Amy's fingers moved automatically over the keys as she stared blindly at the screen. Yet even now he hadn't moved, was still waiting, as if expecting her to swivel round on her chair and say, Just kidding.

She hit the keyboard randomly, not caring what mayhem she was causing to her records, just needing him to see that it wasn't going to happen.

Just needing him!

Say something! Don't just stand there, do something!

After a moment she heard him move, but not towards her, not to take her in his arms, to hold her, promise her that he would never leave her again. Instead he turned and headed for the bathroom. Yes, well, he certainly could do with a shave. That was really important. Far more important than her, or their baby.

As the bathroom door snapped shut she slammed her hands down on the keyboard. 'Stupid!' she said, through the wash of tears. 'Stubborn.' She blinked, saw her reflection against the suddenly darkened screen. Overlaying it was a flashing message. 'Fatal error, fatal error...'

She'd been so sure that she'd been getting through to him. When he'd started on the decorating she'd been certain that the reinforced concrete barrier he'd built around his heart was beginning to weaken. When he'd held her, his cheek pressed against the baby they'd made, she'd been so sure that it was about to crack.

The fact that he'd felt it necessary to put the entire world between them had seemed to suggest that he knew it, too.

And a man who'd flown across the Atlantic because he'd heard she'd had an accident had to be feeling something a little deeper than guilt, surely? Guilt could have been dealt with long distance. A phone call would have reassured him.

But it was clear that Jake Hallam was a man with a cast-iron will, and it would take more than her or the baby she was carrying to bend it. Or maybe she'd just been fooling herself all along.

Well, she couldn't complain that he hadn't warned her.

He had. Loud and clear.

And she'd been listening. But she'd heard so much more than the harsh, take-it-or-leave-it words. She'd been listening, not with her head or any of those ordinary, rational senses that alerted the brain to switch to self-preservation mode. She'd been listening with her whole heart, finely tuned instinct and that other, unquantifiable sense that had never before failed her.

They had all agreed that there was a lot more to this

man than fine bone structure, eyes that could melt permafrost and sexual magnetism so powerful that every nerve cell in her body had fallen in, lined up and leapt to attention. Something buried deep had cried out to her.

And she'd seen so much more behind his eyes than hot, velvet-dark desire. Need. A yearning ache to be loved.

Or thought she had.

Holding him as he'd slept, she'd been fooling herself. Whatever had happened to Jake Hallam to make him the way he was had utterly confounded her capacity to ease.

Worse, she'd cracked, demanded answers when he had none. And now she had to make some plans for the weekend, just in case the guilt that kept bringing him back insisted he check...

She had been in control. Totally in control. She'd taught herself to need no one. Falling in love with Jake had changed her, and until this moment she hadn't realised how much.

All those fine words about coping on her own. He hadn't believed her. She'd torn up his cheque, diverted the housekeeper he'd sent to her, but he hadn't been convinced. He was right.

She was the one bending to his idea of this relationship, not the other way around. He had changed her far more than she had changed him.

Well, that was something she could stop right now. She grabbed her stick, stood up, and for a moment couldn't catch her breath to shout, scream. Anything. Then, as she crumpled to the floor, she realised someone had to be making that noise.

Jake shut the bathroom door, leaned back against it. She'd done it. She'd finally called his bluff. Demanded he make a choice. There was to be no more turning up unannounced to help out, no more lively suppers over the kitchen table, no more quiet evenings when all he had to do was look up to see her, reach out a hand to touch her, knowing that she was there.

Not without some declaration of future intent.

He found himself smiling. He'd thought he'd been doing just what he wanted, but he'd been fooling himself. She'd been calling all the shots. She still was…

A dull thud interrupted his thoughts. The sound of something heavy falling. And his heart turned over.

He'd dragged on Amy's robe and wrenched the door open before her yell of pain exploded onto his eardrums, was at her side before Dorothy had started up the stairs. 'Amy, what is it? What happened?' Her mouth was working but no sound was coming out and he turned to Dorothy, hovering in the doorway. 'Call Dr Maitland. And an ambulance. Now!' Amy was tugging at his arm. 'Don't fret, sweetheart. It won't be long. I knew they should have kept you in hospital… Did you hurt yourself when you fell? Your head? Did you—'

'Jake!'

'Ohmigod, it's the baby! The baby's coming early—'

'Jake, shut up and listen!' Amy shouted, tears of pain squeezing from beneath her lids as she tried to make him understand. 'It's the other leg!'

He stared at her, uncomprehending. 'You hurt the other leg when you fell?' he said.

'No, it's cramp, you idiot! I've got cramp!'

'Cramp?' He rocked back on his heels and stared at her. 'Cramp? Is that all?'

'All?' She was in agony and he thought it was nothing? Normally she would stamp and stretch and walk it off. But she needed at least one good leg for that. '*All?*' she yelled, the finely honed control snapping as she lashed out, beating at him with her fist. 'Don't just sit there, do something! Now—'

The word was choked off as he finally realised what she was saying, grabbed hold of her foot and, propping it against his shoulder, pushed down hard against it, rubbing the knotted muscles in her calf with smooth, firm strokes. Eventually, the muscles began to relax and Amy slumped back on the floor, gasping for air.

'Is that better?' he asked anxiously.

'Just peachy, thanks,' she replied, deeply ironic. Then, 'You do a nice line in panic. It's just as well you didn't volunteer to be my prop and mainstay when I go into labour.'

'I'm sorry. I thought...' He continued to massage her calf muscles. 'Or maybe not.'

'Not, I'd say.' She propped herself up on her elbows to look at him. 'You can stop doing that now.'

'A warm bath would help,' Jake suggested, taking no notice. He was enjoying the hands-on therapy to her leg and was in no particular hurry to stop. This was so much easier than words... 'Or a shower, if that would be easier.' He glanced up, met her gaze. 'I'd be happy to share,' he offered. 'Just as a precaution, you understand, in case the cramp returns.'

'I understand,' she said. 'And I appreciate the sacrifice, but I'd rather keep the hippo at the waterhole routine to myself.'

He lifted her beautifully arched foot from his shoulder and kissed her instep with as much ceremony as if it was the hand of a duchess. 'A very pretty hippo,' he said, and would have reached out to run his hand over the smooth curve of her belly. But her cool green gaze

warned him that such liberties were no longer to be tol-
erated. And she was right. It was time for him to put up,
or shut up. He let his hand fall to his side. 'A beautiful
hippo.'

That raised a wry smile. 'Gracious. Charming. But
you still take your shower solo. Sally!' She looked over
his shoulder and he turned to see Dr Sally Maitland
standing in the door.

'What's up here, then?' she said.

'Absolutely nothing. Totally false alarm. I'm really
sorry—'

'Oh, please don't apologise, Amy. I wouldn't have
missed Mr Hallam in his fluffy pink bathrobe for the
world.'

'It's not my—'

'It looks terrific with the designer stubble.'

'Don't tease him, Sally. He's got jet lag.'

Jake stood up. He could take a little teasing; there
were more important things than his dignity. 'Amy had
a fall, Sally.'

'I didn't fall. I just sort of crumpled up.'

'And the screaming?' he enquired. 'You were simply
rehearsing for the big day?'

She glared at him. 'I had cramp and I couldn't do
anything about it. In my place you'd have screamed.'
She turned to Sally Maitland. 'I'm absolutely fine.'

'I'm delighted to hear it. But if you've no objection I
think I'll check on the baby. Since I'm here. No, stay
right where you are.'

She knelt down, got out a small ear trumpet, hoisted
Amy's shirt up, ignoring the muttered, 'This is nice...'
moving it over the baby until she found what she was
looking for.

'Excellent,' she said, after a moment. 'No problems

here.' Then she turned to Jake. 'Do you want to listen in?'

'To the baby's heart?' His own skipped a beat. 'Can I?'

'Be my guest,' she said, oblivious to Amy's 'I don't believe this…' and moved back so that he could take her place at the listening end. 'At the clinic we can put it on audible monitor, but this is good.'

He listened for a moment to the gentle, squishy beating of the baby's heart. 'Not just good, it's amazing,' he said. Then he heard something else. 'What's that?'

Sally listened for a while, then smiled. 'Hiccups.'

'You're kidding?' She shook her head. 'Really?' And he grinned. 'My baby has hiccups?'

Amy waved. 'Hellooo,' she said. 'I'm still here.'

'Maybe we should leave you there,' Sally told her with mock severity. 'I warned you to stay off that knee.'

'I just stood up—'

'And just fell over,' Jake interjected.

Sally intervened. 'Promise to do exactly as you're told and I'll ask Mr Hallam to pick you up and put you back on your bed.' She looked him up and down. 'Pink bathrobe notwithstanding, he looks up to the job.'

'I think he's demonstrated that to everyone's satisfaction,' Amy said through gritted teeth.

'Don't worry, Sally,' he said. 'I'll make sure she behaves herself.'

'I think it's a bit late to be worrying about either of you behaving yourselves. But, whatever you get up to, make sure she stays off that knee,' she said. And departed.

Neither of them moved until the front door slammed shut. Then Jake said, 'Put your arms around my neck and I'll carry you through to your bedroom.'

'I can—'

'Just do it!'

Amy clasped his neck, felt the sinews tighten beneath her hands as he lifted her and then she was in his arms, held close, her arms draped over his broad shoulders. It occurred to her that being independent, capable, in control, had its downside.

Maybe she should just... No. Nothing would induce her to pretend to be a helpless airhead. But there was no reason not to enjoy the moment, and she let her cheek fall against his chest, listening to his heartbeat, a solid counterbeat to her own, as he carried her along the landing.

When he put her down, she felt positively light-headed.

'Are you going to behave yourself and stay there?'

She came within a whisker of a giggle and a Make me. The idea had a great deal to commend it, not least the fact that he'd have to stay right by her side. Day and night.

Maybe she had hit her head when she fell...

'Go and take your shower, Jake,' she said, before she could weaken. 'I'm not going anywhere for a while and you've got to be somewhere else.'

She held her breath. If he went now, that was it. No more fooling herself. For a moment she thought he was going to say something, but instead he raked his fingers through his hair, leaving it standing up in a dishevelled ruff.

'If you're sure. You've got Dorothy—'

'Yes, I've got Dorothy.'

'And I'll be here when the baby arrives—'

'No.'

'You don't want me with you at the birth? I won't be much use, but—'

'No. I don't want you to come back, Jake. Not unless you're planning on staying.'

'Where to, guv?' the taxi driver asked. 'London, is it?'

Jake's head knew he should be in London, dealing with a dozen loose ends he'd left dangling in his crazy dash home. Nothing, no one had ever precipitated that kind of reaction from him before. Business first, second and third. Anything else, anyone else, had always come a poor runner-up. He'd learned his priorities in his cradle. As the runner-up.

There was just one problem with that. He didn't want to go. If Amy had responded to his invitation to double up in the shower, he wouldn't be going. Not today. Not tonight. But he'd still be leaving in the morning and she knew it.

There had been no mistaking her warning glance when he'd reached out on automatic to gently place his palm over the infant lying safe beneath her breast. It had had all the power of a hand-off from a rugby prop forward.

And it had hurt just as much. A warning of how it would feel if he could never return, never touch her, never hold her again. Was that the pain people called love? How could you tell that it was real? That it would last? How could he say the words when he didn't know?

The driver was waiting.

'No. Take me to Maybridge.' Amy was right. A man had to get his priorities right. 'I need to see a man about a cradle.' He took his cellphone from his overnight bag and called Maggie.

'Jake, for heaven's sake, where are you? I've set up a video conference—'

'Maggie,' he said, cutting her off. 'Do you remember that conversation we had about what would happen if ever I happened to fall under a bus?'

'I was speaking metaphorically.'

'Well, metaphorically, it's just happened.'

'Oh. Oh, I see. Well, you sound in remarkably good spirits, considering,' she said, laughing. 'How do you feel?'

'In shock. Put back the video conference an hour and call a meeting for this evening, will you? I've got anything up to eight weeks to change my life.'

And make a cradle.

Dorothy put down the iron as Amy walked slowly into the kitchen, leaning on her stick. 'Mr Hallam isn't staying for dinner?'

'No, Dorothy. He's gone back to London. For good.'

'Oh, my dear...'

'And, much as I'll miss you, I'm afraid it's time for you to go too.'

CHAPTER NINE

NINTH MONTH. Nearly there! The baby's head should drop into the pelvis ready for the birth so you can breathe a little more easily. Which is good. You may have a tendency to 'leak'. Which is not. And there may be Braxton Hicks contractions to add a little extra uncertainty to your life.

AMY had been joking about looking like a hippopotamus. A big mistake. She didn't only look like one, she felt like one. She was slow and ungainly and, although she hadn't seen them for some time, she just knew her ankles were swollen.

Her knee wasn't enjoying all the extra weight, either. She'd never take the simple act of running up and down stairs for granted ever again. Dorothy had warned her, but she'd refused to listen.

Well, she'd been refusing to listen for months. No more fooling herself. She'd given Jake an ultimatum and he'd made his choice. And she could take care of herself.

Big joke. Just getting cereals and orange juice for breakfast was hard work.

She perched on a kitchen chair that no longer seemed large enough to encompass her bottom, sipped her orange juice and immediately needed to visit the bathroom. As she made her way slowly upstairs, she finally admitted that Jake was right about extending the house.

With the growing baby making even the most basic call of nature an increasingly frequent, if mostly unpro-

169

ductive nuisance, a downstairs lavatory was fast rising to number three on her wish list.

She wanted her body back!

She wanted Jake.

She opened the nursery door, reminding herself how much he'd cared, how far he'd come from the man who'd thought a cheque would get him off the father-hood hook. He'd read the books, bought magazines, knew as much about what a baby needed as she did. Maybe more.

She fumbled in her pocket, took out her phone and, abandoning all pride, she called his office, asked to speak to him.

'Miss Jones? Maggie Simons, Jake's secretary. Can I help?'

'He's not there?'

'No, I thought...' She stopped. 'Is it urgent? Can I give him a message if he phones? The baby's due very soon, isn't it?'

'I certainly hope so.'

'Is there anything I can do?'

'No, but thanks for offering. No need to tell Jake I called. There's no message.' And she hung up.

Maggie didn't immediately replace the receiver. In front of her she had the final account from the Garland Agency for the services of Dorothy Fuller, awaiting her signature. It was a month in arrears and had come the slow way from the accounts department. The house-keeper had left Upper Haughton nearly seven weeks ago. And if Jake wasn't there, it meant that Amy Jones was on her own.

She could try Jake's mobile, leave a message, ask him what he wanted to do about it. Or she could call Dorothy Fuller and find out what the devil was going on. It required an executive decision. Since she was the only executive available, she made one.

Amy snapped the little cellphone shut. That was it. She blinked back a sudden wash of tears. No point in crying. Crying for Jake was like crying for the moon.

She could have had him if she'd been prepared to compromise, take him on his terms. Instead, she'd stubbornly stuck to her own. All or nothing. If he'd finally got the message and chosen 'nothing' it would be pitiful to complain that she was lonely.

Even her baby, too cramped now for aerobics, was quiet. With a sigh, she picked up Jake's poetry book and, settling on the futon, began to read out loud.

'You've done a great job.' Mike ran his hand over the cradle. 'If you ever want to give up the corporate high-wire, I'll take you on as an apprentice any time.'

Jake grinned. 'That's a compliment, isn't it?'

'You bet.'

'Well, thanks for the after-hours loan of your workshop. I'm sorry I've been under your feet for so long.'

'You're welcome. But you look tired. You should go home to Amy and let her wrap you in a little loving care.'

'I had to get my life in order. Finish this. I couldn't have done this without you. Wouldn't have known where to start.'

'If I'd left you to your own devices your baby would be at school, along with any number of little brothers and sisters, by the time it was finished.'

'Brothers and sisters?' Mike's only response was to gently rock the cradle. 'You haven't told Amy about this, have you? I want it to be a surprise.'

'Your secret is safe with me. But you're running out of time.'

'I know. I'd better get on. Run me through the finishing process again.'

'Finishing is what really takes the time,' Mike said, taking a sheet of finest sandpaper from the rack. 'Time and love.'

'Love?'

'What else? Isn't that why you chose to make the cradle yourself, rather than buying an antique?'

'Amy! What on earth are you doing here?' Vicki exclaimed. 'The baby's due in a week. You should be at home with your feet up.'

'At home staring at four walls while my neighbours take it in turn to call in and "keep me company" on a rota basis? I need something to do before I go crazy.

'You could knit.'

'I've got calluses from knitting. And it's not my fingers I need to keep busy. It's my mind.'

'Believe me, sitting with your feet up being made a fuss of will seem like bliss in retrospect when you're being kept awake all night by a crying baby.'

'Oh, thanks. As if the entire neighbourhood pitying me for a poor abandoned woman isn't enough, you have to pile on the agony.'

'Abandoned?' Vicki frowned. 'What do you mean, abandoned? Jake's with you, isn't he? I mean, I saw him this morning at Mike's workshop. I've seen him there most mornings this week. We've been rushed off our feet because of the holiday, and I've been coming in early—' Amy, who had taken an instant dislike to a display of candles and was twitchily rearranging it, lost

control of her fingers and they crashed to the floor.
Neither of them moved. 'You didn't know?'

'No. I haven't seen him since he came racing back
from the States when Willow told him about my stupid
accident. He said he'd try to get back, but, hell, Vicki,
if it was that hard—'

'You told him not to bother?'

'No. I told him I had other plans.'

'And he believed you?'

'I've no idea. I decided I needed a weekend of pam-
pering at a health farm and I took Willow along for
company.' She shrugged. 'Actually, I told him not to
come back at all, unless he planned to stay. I didn't want
to become just another one of those loose ends he had
to tie up.' Loose ends he'd had time to plait, splice, tie
up in a fancy Turk's Head knot. Apparently he'd been
doing it in Mike's workshop. She'd thought Mike was
a friend. And Willow must have known, too. She bent
to pick up the fallen candles.

'Leave it, Amy, I'll do it.'

'No, I can manage. The baby's head's dropped and I
can bend again. Well, after a fashion.' And anything was
better than confronting Vicki's sympathy. 'Is he there
now? Jake?' What did pride matter?

'He left about half an hour ago.'

'Not that you were taking any particular notice.'

'It would have been hard to miss him. He backed that
yellow estate up to the side door. He and Mike loaded
something into it. I don't know what it was, though.
He'd put a sheet over it.'

'How like a man. The entire courtyard were doubtless
hanging out of their doors and windows—'

'In December? You've got to be kidding.' Vicki took

the candles from her, helped her to her feet. 'Go and sit down. I'll call a taxi to take you home.'

'No.' She straightened. Eased her back. 'I've booked a pick-up for five o'clock, but don't worry, I won't get under your feet. I'm going to turn out my office.'

'What?'

'I'm restless, need something to do. I was going to turn out the cupboards at home, but Dorothy left them fit for a centre spread in one of those lifestyle magazines.'

'Oh, I see. You're nesting.' Vicki bit down on her lip to keep from smiling. 'Well, don't overdo it. Not unless you're planning on giving birth on your desk. We'll be here if you need anything.'

She was exhausted. Her knee was aching, the niggling ache in her back was getting unbearable. She'd done exactly what everyone had told her not to do. Too much. But as the taxi pulled into the lane everything suddenly changed. The cottage light was on.

Jake! It had to be Jake. He was back, and the aches fell away from her and the world was a vivid, wonderful place again.

She burst through the back door, her heart on her sleeve, determined not to leave him in the slightest doubt about how glad she was to see him. No more take-all-the-time-you-need, no more holding him at arm's length with her I-can-wait, Miss-Cool-as-a-cucumber act. She wasn't cool, she was hot, sizzling hot, and she couldn't wait another moment. She wanted him, needed him, loved him and it was time to put her own heart on the line and let him know.

'Jake?' She kicked off her boots in the mud room and pushed open the kitchen door. Dorothy, her face slightly flushed, hands floury, looked up from the kitchen table and smiled.

'Hello, dear. I'm just making an apple crumble. When you weren't here, I popped in to see Mrs Cook and she gave me some lovely Bramleys...' She spread the topping over a dish of stewed apple. 'You go in and settle yourself by the fire and get warmed through. I'll have a cup of tea for you in a minute.'

'Dorothy...' Disappointment temporarily glued her throat. 'What on earth are you doing here? I thought you'd be working for someone else by now.'

'I've had offers, but nothing that tempted me. At my time of life I pick and choose my jobs. I like to be really needed. Of course, Maggie, Jake's secretary—' she covered the crumble and put it in the fridge, then reached for the kettle '—insisted you really needed me. She offered me a very nice little bonus.'

Not Jake? He'd left it to his secretary? 'Dorothy—'

'It was a pity I had to turn her down, but I'd already decided to retire, you see. I've sold my house and I'm buying that little cottage at the end of the lane. This is such a friendly village.' She set the kettle on top of the Aga. 'The paperwork went through today.'

For a moment Amy believed her. Then she said, 'You told me you live with your son and daughter-in-law and you take these little jobs to get out from under their feet.'

'Did I? Oh, dear, I'd forgotten that. You won't tell Maggie, will you? She thought it was such a clever idea to buy the cottage so that I could be near you.' She wiped up a few stray crumbs. 'And I do so irritate Susie, with my fussing.'

'Maybe, but I bet she's always glad to see you back.' And Amy hugged her. 'I am. The village hasn't been the same without you.' But her pleasure in Dorothy's return couldn't compete with her disappointment. For one blissful moment she had thought that everything was going to be all right. Now, the low ache in her back returned with a vengeance, every pound of extra weight dragging at her.

'There's a casserole in the oven, any time you're ready.'

'I'm not hungry just now. Maybe later.'

'Right, well, you go and put your feet up. I'll bring you a cup of tea and then I'll get off. I'm playing bridge at the vicarage tonight.'

'Better wear a bullet-proof vest, then.' She had just reached the hall when something occurred to her. 'Dorothy? How did you get in?'

'I let her in.'

For a moment she thought she heard Jake, could swear that he was behind her, that she could feel his breath on her neck.

She was hallucinating. That was it. She'd spent the day cleaning every corner of her office and she'd overdone it. And she'd just experienced giddy euphoria followed almost instantly by deep-in-her-boots disappointment. Her blood pressure was probably through the roof and she was hearing things.

'Dorothy?' she repeated.

'You shouldn't have sent her away.' Amy spun round. She wasn't just hearing things, she was seeing them... Jake reached behind her, closed the kitchen door. 'Not without telling me. If I'd known you were alone—' He broke off.

'You'd have had to waste time worrying about me?' she enquired archly. Archly! Five minutes ago she'd been promising herself that she'd stop playing games, would fling herself into his arms and tell him that he lit up her life.

A moment ago she'd thought her heart was in her boots. She knew nothing.

'Oh, damn!' She stopped, caught her breath, closing her eyes as the muscles of her uterus contracted.

'What is it?' He was right behind her, his hand about her shoulders.

She shook her head. 'Nothing. Braxton Hicks contractions. It's just—'

'Just the body going through a practice lap. I know.'

'Of course you do. You read about it in a book,' she snapped.

'You've had them before?'

'Yes, Jake,' she said, shaking him off. 'I know what I'm talking about so there's no need to panic. I'm not about to have the baby on the living room floor.'

'I wish I'd been to all the antenatal classes with you. I should have been there.'

'You're a busy man with more important things to worry about.'

But Jake refused to be pushed away, reaching for her, wrapping his arms about her, holding her. 'There is nothing more important. You think I don't worry about you?' He looked down at her, his expression deadly serious as he pushed her floppy fringe back from her face. 'Every minute of the day and night?'

'Where *were* you, Jake? What have you been doing?'

'Making myself dispensable. Putting my affairs in order. Tying up loose ends. I'm going to need a lot of time in the coming weeks, months, years if I'm going to be the kind of father I want to be. Where were you today? I arrived bearing gifts to find the house dark and cold. Why did you send Dorothy away?'

'Because.' She frowned. 'You didn't know?'

'Not until an hour ago or I'd have done something about it sooner. Thankfully, Maggie was on the ball.'

'She really bought a house?'

'In less than a week. Pretty good going, eh?' He grinned. 'The estate agent must have wondered what had hit him. Where have you been?'

'Nowhere. Just cleaning out my office.'

'Nesting?'

'Piffle. Apparently I just missed you at Mike's place. What were you doing there?'

'I'll show you.' He pushed open the living room door. 'Come and put your feet up. Get warm.'

The fire was bright, stingingly bright. Something must be making her eyes sting. She blinked furiously. 'What the...?' She stopped, looked back at him uncertainly. 'You bought that cradle? The one we looked at?'

'No.'

She took a step into the room. No, it wasn't the same. The firelight gleamed off the silky glow of polished oak. 'Another one, then...'

'Do you remember what you said that day?'

She was flustered, uncertain. Jake was different, somehow. Less tense. His eyes were softer... 'I don't know. Something about a man searching out the perfect tree, felling it—' She stopped, looked back. 'Don't tell me you've been out in the greenwoods with your trusty axe?'

'No. Apparently any decent-sized oak would have had a preservation order on it. And it takes a long time to season the wood. But I did choose the timber, and with Mike's help I cut it. It looks simple enough, but it took weeks to make.'

'*You* made this?'

'For you. For our baby.'

Our baby. The words sounded so sweet. She crossed the room, touched the hood, setting the cradle gently rocking. Knelt down beside it, laid her cheek to the smooth wood, breathing in the scent of beeswax, touching the white linen waiting for a new life, and she sucked her lips hard back against her teeth.

'You do it every time, Jake Hallam. You take me to the brink and I think, This is it, Amy Jones, you've messed it all up and he's never coming back. And then you do something else to take my breath away.' She felt another contraction, stronger than before, a smooth ripple of muscle like a strong wave passing over her. She waited a moment, breathing with it until it had passed. 'Is that how you do business?' she said. 'Drive your customers crazy? Make them desperate, bring them to their knees?'

'I'm the one on my knees, Amy. Asking you if you can ever forgive me for being so stubborn, so stupid.' He knelt beside her, took her hand.

Dorothy bustled in with a tea tray that she set down on a low table. 'The casserole is in the warming oven. Put the crumble in when you dish up and it'll be ready. There's cream in the fridge. And don't worry about the washing up; I'll be back first thing in the morning.'

'Thank you, Dorothy.' Neither of them spoke until they heard the door shut. 'Tea?' she asked.

'The only thing I want is you.' And after a moment, sweetly hesitant, he kissed her. Gently, tenderly, lovingly, holding her as if she was made of eggshells. Far too briefly. 'Bad timing,' he said, as another contraction swept over her.

'There's no bad time to fall in love,' she said when it had passed, light years from cool, or arch or snappy.

She leaned back, nestling her head against his shoulder, tucking his arms under hers so that he could rest his hands on her abdomen, feel the coming contraction.

'Should we do something about that?' he asked. 'Tell someone?'

'Not yet. There's plenty of time.' She closed her eyes, wanting to prolong this time, knowing that it was special. 'I was born here. In this house. It belonged to my grandmother.'

'You came here after your family were killed?'

'Yes.'

'I know so little about you.' He rubbed his cheek against her hair.

'More than I know about you. Where were you born, Jake?'

'Not like this, in front of a warm log fire. My mother would have thought this very...rustic.'

'Oh?'

He held her close. 'She favoured a famously expensive nursing home, where I could be delivered into the lap of luxury with the minimum inconvenience to all concerned.' She turned and looked at him. 'Neglect isn't confined to the disadvantaged, Amy.'

'Was your father there? When you were born?'

'My father, a man who had his priorities very firmly fixed on the important things in life, was in Hong Kong on business. I not only look like him, I learned at a very early age that I was just like him.'

'No.'

'Yes, Amy. But then I had a double dose of genetic single-mindednesss. My mother engaged a maternity nanny and joined him a week later.'

'She left you behind?'

'I wasn't a commercial asset.'

She reached up, covered his hand with her own. 'Why? If she didn't want a baby... If he didn't...'

'Oh, he did. All that money, property, required a suitable heir. He discovered too late that children are the downside of fatherhood. Messy, uncontrollable. And, no matter how much you distance yourself, a small boy who is desperate for attention can wreak havoc.'

'Well, I should hope so.'

'I wasn't a nice little boy, Amy. Wheeled out by a nanny to be admired by my parents' influential friends, I discovered that repeating a new word I'd overheard was a real conversation-stopper. And that being bad got me a lot more attention than being good ever had.'

She flinched. 'I'm sorry...so sorry...'

'Anything was better than being ignored.' He shrugged. 'Of course, it only precipitated my early entry into the boarding school system.'

'You hated it?'

'Not particularly. Only the fact that my parents were always too busy to come to open days. To fetch me home for weekends. As soon as I learned that "I'll try..." meant nothing, I became very inventive at getting my parents summoned to school. I was expelled from three prep schools for disruptive behaviour in rapid succession and then, when I wanted to ensure my father's presence at my tenth birthday party, I took his brand-new Mercedes and drove it into a tree. Just to be sure he couldn't leave.'

'Were you hurt?'

'No, but inevitably the police became involved, and the family court. My mother sat there and wept, telling them how much she loved me, how she'd tried, that it broke her heart to let me go but there was nothing more she could do. The heads of three distinguished prep schools wrote letters to back her up and I was taken into the care and protection of the state.'

'Oh, Jake.'

'I didn't learn for a long time. I still thought that if I behaved badly enough, they'd finally realise how much I needed them.'

'They didn't come.'

'No. That was it. They wrote me off like a bad debt. I was lucky. I ended up with Aunt Lucy. I could have—' Amy gasped. 'Sweetheart?'

'I think this is the real thing.'

'I'll call Sally and let her know that things are underway.' He got to his feet, helped her up. 'Hold on to the back of the sofa, lean forward and it'll help,' he said.

'Know-all,' Amy said, and grinned as he rang the doctor and the midwife.

'Do you want me to call Willow?' he asked.

'Sally's on her way, and the midwife, and you're here, Jake, a walking encyclopaedia on the subject of childbirth...' She grasped his hand as she was seized by a more powerful contraction. 'Leave Willow to enjoy her evening. We're doing okay.'

'Are we?'

'Scared?' she asked.

'Petrified.' He'd stepped off the cliff and he hadn't reached the bottom yet. But that was simply life; a plunge in the dark. If you were lucky, a hand was waiting to grasp yours as you passed so that you weren't alone. Amy had been waiting too long for him to reach out for hers. He'd so nearly missed her... 'But we're in this together,' he said, with a smile. 'Til death us do part.' Then, 'Shouldn't I be timing those contractions?'

She smiled, kissed him. 'Any time you're ready.' Then, 'Jake, what changed your mind? You said you were like your father. What happened to change your mind?'

'You.' He took her hands, held them together against his chest. 'He'd have written a cheque, just like me, but when you sent it back he'd have shrugged, called you a fool and thrown the bits in the bin, along with the boo-tees, then wiped the incident from his memory—'

'Bootees? What bootees?'

'The pink ones.' He felt in his pocket, found them. 'They're a bit grubby.'

'I wondered what had happened to those.'

'You put them in the envelope with the torn-up cheque.'

She shook her head. 'Not me. Vicki must have re-opened the envelope and put them in before she gave it to the courier. She was nauseatingly gooey that day, hav-ing been swept off her feet by the leather-clad motorbike rider who delivered your unwelcome missive.' She caught her breath. 'You've been had, Jake,' she said, when the contraction had passed. 'Suckered.' She grinned. 'Have you really been carrying them about with you for all these months?'

'Yes. I suppose I should have given them back, but since you're having a boy you won't be needing them.'

'It's a girl,' she replied stubbornly, and then let out a surprised yell as another contraction coincided with the ringing of the front doorbell. 'And I'm about to prove it.'

'He's beautiful, Jake.' They were finally alone. The mid-wife gone, Sally dashing away to catch a little sleep before morning surgery. Amy looked from her baby to Jake. 'Thank you so much.'

'You like him? You're not disappointed?'

'He's adorable. Absolutely perfect.'

'Only I thought…'

'Mmm?' She touched George's tiny hand with her finger and he gripped it tightly.

'We could always try again.'

She kissed her infant, then looked up. 'You're a comedian, Jake Hallam.'

'No. I'm serious. I want you to have your little girl.' He kissed her. 'George should have a sister. Boys need sisters to keep them in line and I just want you to know that I'm prepared to keep trying for as long as you are—'

'That's very obliging of you.'

'But you'll have to make an honest man of me first. I'm going to have to insist that you marry me.'

'Insist?' She was trying very hard not to smile. It was a waste of time.

'All right. Beg. Implore. Beseech you to marry me. You've been extraordinarily patient. You've kept telling me to go away and I thought I wanted to.'

'So why did you keep coming back?'

'I don't know. Didn't know. It made me so angry.'

'I noticed.'

'I thought "love" was just a meaningless word.'

'The way your parents used it.'

'They were so wrong. But it doesn't matter now. I know what love is. I know that the power of true love is so strong that it can heal the soul.' He pressed her hand to his forehead, closed his eyes, stretching for the words. 'You've shown me that I'm not bound by the past. That the past doesn't matter. That I can be anyone I want to be. I was here today—not in some meeting, not on the other side of the world. I helped to deliver my son, made with the woman I love more than life itself. That's the man I want to be, Amy.'

He waited a moment, but when there was no reply he looked up and saw that she'd drifted off. It didn't matter. He'd tell her again tomorrow. And the day after. For as long as it took.

And he lifted baby George from his mother's arms, tucking the fine shawl about him before kissing him, holding him for a while, then settling him in the cradle he'd brought up and put beside the bed.

Then he turned back to Amy, kissed her, too, pulled the cover over her shoulders. She sighed, stirred. Opened her eyes. Murmured something sleepily.

He bent closer. 'What was that?'

'You guarantee we'll get a girl next time?'

'I'll try...' He stopped, then saw that she was smiling. 'I guarantee that it will be a baby,' he said. And he took her hand and made a cross against his heart. Then he took out the ring box that had been burning a hole in his pocket since he'd picked it up at the jeweller the day before. He opened it, took out the diamond ring and slipped it on her finger. 'I love you, Amy Jones.' He liked the feel of the word in his mouth so much that he said it again. 'I love you.'

EPILOGUE

'LOOK this way, George!' The five-year-old, dark like his father, green glints inherited from his mother flashing in his eyes, turned for the camera. 'Okay, you can cut it...now!'

George snipped carefully through the gold ribbon tied across the door of the hundredth 'Amaryllis Jones' store, and as a big cheer went up from the crowd gathered on the pavement Jake retrieved the scissors and gathered up his son.

'Well done, George!'

'Can I have some cake now?' he asked.

'Absolutely. Look, there's Granny Lucy; she'll get you some. Take James with you.'

'What about Mark?'

'He's a bit little for cake. Next time, maybe.' Jake glanced at Amy. 'Congratulations, sweetheart. A hundred stores in five years.'

'A hundred stores and three babies.'

'Three boys.'

'Three gorgeous boys,' she said. 'Adorable boys. Just like their father.'

'Still no Polly, though.'

'Well, actually...' Amy's shoulders shifted very slightly. 'I was talking to Lucy.'

'Oh?'

'She's been asked if she could take in an abandoned newborn baby girl, but, well, she's getting on a bit and she just doesn't think she can cope. The thing is, there's just no one else…so she suggested us.'

'As foster parents?'

'Would you mind?'

For a moment Jake seemed slightly stunned. Then he shook his head. 'No. I think it's a wonderful idea.' He took their smallest boy from her, put his arm about her and kissed her. 'But don't think I won't still be making every possible effort to provide you with a daughter of your own.'

'You're all talk,' Amy said, with a slow green glance from her bewitching eyes.

Nothing had changed. Nearly six years had passed since the day they'd met and still she could stop his heart with a look.

'I'll show you the difference between talk and action the minute I have you to myself, Amy Hallam.'

She laughed. 'Promises, promises.'

His only answer was to take her hand in his and draw a cross over his heart.

What happens when you suddenly
discover your happy twosome is about
to be turned into a...*family?*
Do you laugh?
Do you cry?
Or...do you get married?

The answer is all of the above—and plenty more!

Share the laughter and the tears with
Harlequin Romance® as these
unsuspecting couples have to be

When parenthood takes you by surprise!

THE BACHELOR'S BABY
Liz Fielding (August, #3666)

CLAIMING HIS BABY
Rebecca Winters (October, #3673)

HER HIRED HUSBAND
Renee Roszel (December, #3681)

Available wherever Harlequin books are sold.

If you enjoyed what you just read,
then we've got an offer you can't resist!

Take 2 bestselling love stories FREE!

Plus get a FREE surprise gift!

Clip this page and mail it to Harlequin Reader Service®

IN U.S.A.
3010 Walden Ave.
P.O. Box 1867
Buffalo, N.Y. 14240-1867

IN CANADA
P.O. Box 609
Fort Erie, Ontario
L2A 5X3

YES! Please send me 2 free Harlequin Romance® novels and my free surprise gift. After receiving them, if I don't wish to receive anymore, I can return the shipping statement marked cancel. If I don't cancel, I will receive 6 brand-new novels every month, before they're available in stores! In the U.S.A., bill me at the bargain price of $3.15 plus 25¢ shipping & handling per book and applicable sales tax, if any*. In Canada, bill me at the bargain price of $3.59 plus 25¢ shipping & handling per book and applicable taxes**. That's the complete price and a savings of 10% off the cover prices—what a great deal! I understand that accepting the 2 free books and gift places me under no obligation ever to buy any books. I can always return a shipment and cancel at any time. Even if I never buy another book from Harlequin, the 2 free books and gift are mine to keep forever.

186 HEN DC7K
386 HEN DC7L

Name _____ (PLEASE PRINT)

Address _____ Apt.# _____

City _____ State/Prov. _____ Zip/Postal Code _____

* Terms and prices subject to change without notice. Sales tax applicable in N.Y.
** Canadian residents will be charged applicable provincial taxes and GST.
   All orders subject to approval. Offer limited to one per household and not valid to current Harlequin Romance® subscribers.
   ® are registered trademarks of Harlequin Enterprises Limited.

HROM01   ©2001 Harlequin Enterprises Limited

Harlequin invites you to walk down the aisle...

To honor our year long celebration of weddings, we are offering an exciting opportunity for you to own the Harlequin Bride Doll. Handcrafted in fine bisque porcelain, the wedding doll is dressed for her wedding day in a cream satin gown accented by lace trim. She carries an exquisite traditional bridal bouquet and wears a cathedral length dotted Swiss veil. Embroidered flowers cascade down her lace overskirt to the scalloped hemline; underneath all is a multi-layered crinoline.

Join us in our celebration of weddings by sending away for your own Harlequin Bride Doll. This doll regularly retails for $74.95 U.S./approx. $108.68 CDN. One doll per household. Requests must be received no later than December 31, 2001. Offer good while quantities of gifts last. Please allow 6-8 weeks for delivery. Offer good in the U.S. and Canada only. Become part of this exciting offer!

Simply complete the order form and mail to:
"A Walk Down the Aisle"

IN U.S.A	IN CANADA
P.O. Box 9057	P.O. Box 622
3010 Walden Ave.	Fort Erie, Ontario
Buffalo, NY 14269-9057	L2A 5X3

Enclosed are eight (8) proofs of purchase found in the last pages of every specially marked Harlequin series book and $3.75 check or money order (for postage and handling). Please send my Harlequin Bride Doll to:

_____
Name (PLEASE PRINT)

_____
Address   Apt. #

_____
City   State/Prov.   Zip/Postal Code

_____
Account # (if applicable)   **097 KIK DAEW**

HARLEQUIN®
Makes any time special ®

Visit us at www.eHarlequin.com

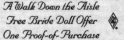

A Walk Down the Aisle
Free Bride Doll Offer
One Proof-of-Purchase

PHWDAPOPR2

COMING SOON...

AN EXCITING OPPORTUNITY TO SAVE ON THE PURCHASE OF HARLEQUIN AND SILHOUETTE BOOKS!

DETAILS TO FOLLOW IN OCTOBER 2001!

YOU WON'T WANT TO MISS IT!

PHQ401

THE  AUSTRALIANS

MEN WHO TURN
YOUR WHOLE WORLD
UPSIDE DOWN!

Look out for novels about the Wonder from
Down Under—where spirited women win the
hearts of Australia's most eligible men.

Harlequin Romance®:

OUTBACK WITH THE BOSS
Barbara Hannay (September, #3670)

MASTER OF MARAMBA
Margaret Way (October, #3671)

OUTBACK FIRE
Margaret Way (December, #3678)

Harlequin Presents®:

A QUESTION OF MARRIAGE
Lindsay Armstrong (October, #2208)

FUGITIVE BRIDE
Miranda Lee (November, #2212)

Available wherever Harlequin books are sold.

 HARLEQUIN®
Makes any time special ®